Sherlock Holmes and the Adventure of the Elusive Ear

by

David MacGregor

Paperback ISBN 978-1-78705-709-8
ePub ISBN 978-1-78705-710-4
PDF ISBN 978-1-78705-711-1

Published by Orange Pip Books
335 Princess Park Manor, Royal Drive,
London, N11 3GX
www.orangepipbooks.com

Cover design by Brian Belanger

For Louise

Acknowledgments

This story, along with its companion pieces, "Sherlock Holmes and the Adventure of the Fallen Soufflé" and "Sherlock Holmes and the Adventure of the Ghost Machine," began life as a play at The Purple Rose Theatre Company in Chelsea, Michigan. First and foremost, my eternal thanks goes to my friend and colleague Guy Sanville, who directed "Elusive Ear," and always pushes me to make the story better. My gratitude also goes towards the dozens of talented and highly skilled collaborators who made these plays successful. And of course, my thanks to actor, playwright, composer, and musician Jeff Daniels for founding The Purple Rose Theatre Company in 1991 and providing a home for innumerable artists.

Special thanks goes to Hope Shangle, who offered an attentive ear and thoughtful insights over coffee and pastries, then volunteered her considerable web wizard talents as needed. Thanks also to the Amateur Mendicant Society of Detroit and Holmesian guru Howard Ostrom, whose enthusiasm for this new version of Sherlock Holmes was deeply appreciated. My brother Iain MacGregor and good friend Peter Morris were kind enough to cast a careful eye over the text, and I am extremely grateful to Steve Emecz, Richard Ryan, and the team at MX Publishing for gracefully ushering these stories into a different medium and giving them an entirely new audience.

Finally, a deep and heartfelt bow to Sir Arthur Conan Doyle for creating, as Vincent Starrett poetically expressed it, "two men of note who never lived and so can never die."

Contents

Introduction

Irene Adler was not dead. There. I've said it. Yes, I am well aware that I had pronounced her quite dead and gone in "A Scandal in Bohemia," but that, I'm afraid, was an outright lie. Similarly, readers of delicate and chronologically obsessed constitutions should brace themselves for the revelation that at the time this story took place, in late 1888, Professor Moriarty was already dead. Yes, in "The Final Problem" I declared that his demise took place at the Reichenbach Falls in 1891, but that was at the behest of Holmes, who always seemed anxious to muddy the details of his final encounter with the Professor (my offhand comment regarding the unlikelihood of an elderly Professor of Mathematics wrestling Holmes at the edge of the Falls had been met with a cold stare).

Should the reader care to excoriate me for such ungentlemanly behaviour, I assure you I am quite past caring. By this point in time I am mouldering away quite nicely in this or that graveyard, which is the only reason that I am now allowing this particular tale to come to light. So then, the machinations of the Professor will not intrude upon this story at all, although his influence was not, shall we say, entirely unfelt. On the other hand, should the reader wonder why I consigned Miss Adler to oblivion, simply read on and all shall be made clear.

In the first place, as anyone with an ounce of common sense must have realised, Sherlock Holmes and Miss Adler were mutually smitten practically from the moment they laid eyes on one another. It wasn't anything so commonplace as a general romantic feeling or the stirring of more primal urges; no, it seemed to be an instant recognition that the world was a better and more interesting place with each other in it. It was there in the way they looked at one another, the way they both fought to keep a small smile off their faces, and the way they spoke to one another like two ancient souls who had spent many previous lifetimes together and had somehow, amidst the roiling sea of humanity, found one another once again. Although they made an unlikely pair, the instinctive connection between the London detective and the opera singer from New Jersey was as immediate as it was profound.

So it was that when all of the details of "A Scandal in Bohemia" were nicely tidied up and the King of Bohemia had been despatched back to his native land to live a life of well-dressed official uselessness, Miss Adler moved into 221B Baker Street and took up residence with us. I'm afraid that I still retain enough of a Victorian sensibility to blush slightly as I write those words, but that was the cold, hard reality of it. Holmes and Miss Adler had found one another, they were going to be together, and that was that. It was thus left up to me, the narrator of the tales, to somehow make sense of this curious *ménage a trois* in a manner that would not outrage the delicate sensibilities of the British reading public and the admirers of Mr. Sherlock Holmes.

This I endeavoured to do to the best of my ability, although I will not pretend that there weren't some uncomfortable moments from time to time. Still, in retrospect I can say that living in the company of Holmes and Miss Adler was well worth any occasional inconvenience or awkward situation. Considered separately, they were both utterly remarkable individuals possessed of a dazzling array of interests and abilities. Together, they were simply transcendent. I do not expect the reader to take me at my word on this claim, and so, let me demonstrate by relating the remarkable story of "The Adventure of the Elusive Ear."

This was one of several tales that I was, shall we say, encouraged to keep from the public so long as all of the principals were still living. These tales involved individuals of significant historical note and importance, and at the time they occurred I was not inclined to sully or besmirch anyone's reputation, as well as being mindful of the unpleasant world of lawyers and libel lawsuits. There was also the fact that too many revelations would be detrimental to the respect and deference Sherlock Holmes required to conduct his consulting practice to the best of his abilities.

Nevertheless, these cases are some of the most remarkable that we ever encountered, and I would be remiss if I did not set them down so that future generations would be able to appreciate the full scope of the powers of my friend, Sherlock Holmes. Aside from the story you now hold in your hand, I also plan on relating at least two other astonishing tales—"The Adventure of the Fallen Soufflé" and "The Adventure of the Ghost Machine." I shall compose these stories as my health and schedule permit, and then transfer them to my despatch box at Cox and Company for what I hope will be the delight and edification of posterity.

But first, a little housekeeping to explain our living arrangements. I am aware that there has been much speculation as to just how many wives I had over the years, and the answer to that is quite simple—zero. Mary Morstan and I? Another ruse, I'm afraid, concocted in my efforts to get the reading public interested in the exploits of Sherlock Holmes. After my first Sherlock Holmes novel, "A Study in Scarlet," had sunk without a trace, in my second effort, "The Sign of the Four," I endeavoured to appeal to female readers a bit more by fabricating a romance between Mary Morstan and myself, a fictional courtship which naturally enough ended in a fictional wedding. This was done with the full cooperation of Miss Morstan (not her real name, of course), aided and abetted by a crisp fifty-pound note. What can I say? I was desperate.

I was quite certain that the unique and fascinating tales of Sherlock Holmes would appeal to the reading public, but I was mindful not only of the failure of "A Study in Scarlet," but also the lack of public interest in Edgar Allan Poe's quite innovative detective stories written some fifty years earlier—"The Murders in the Rue Morgue" and "The Purloined Letter." When I first read these stories I was swept away by the cleverness of the narrative and the intelligence of Poe's protagonist, Monsieur Dupin.

Here, I felt, was a truly modern hero, one whose heroism wasn't measured by his body count or romantic conquests. Instead, living within the chaos of a modern metropolis, Poe gave his readers a detective who could restore sense and order to the world by explaining the apparently inexplicable. And yet, the public didn't exactly clamour for more stories featuring Dupin, and Poe seemed to lose interest in the character and detective stories in general, immersing himself more and more in rather gruesome and unpleasant tales that seemed indicative of an increasingly unhealthy state of mind in the author.

It wasn't as if detectives completely disappeared from literature after that. There were the rather long-winded tales of Émile Gaboriau, featuring Monsieur Lecoq, who was based on the real-life thief and detective Eugène François Vidocq, founder of the French Sûreté. These enjoyed a brief vogue, but then poor Gaboriau passed away at the young age of forty. In

England, well-respected authors like Dickens and Wilkie Collins had included detectives in their novels, but the detectives were never the central characters, and much like Collins' rose-loving Sergeant Cuff in "The Moonstone," invariably quite useless. It occurred to me that perhaps mysteries in and of themselves might not be enough to attract a dedicated readership, so I hoped that including my "courtship" and "marriage" within a Sherlock Holmes story would turn the tide in my favour.

I even maintained this fiction for the first few Sherlock Holmes short stories, with Holmes and I supposedly living separately and just happening to see one another before launching into the actual mystery. Thankfully, I had a talk with George Newnes, the publisher of "The Strand Magazine," where my short Sherlock Holmes tales had created an immediate sensation, and he assured me that based on the enthusiastic letters he was receiving from readers, no one was remotely interested in my "wife," and I was free to get rid of her at the earliest opportunity, which I thereupon did with a sigh of relief. This simplified the structure of the stories wonderfully. Holmes and I were confirmed bachelors who lived together and ventured out into London and the surrounding countryside on various adventures, with no wives or children to muck up the proceedings.

Finally, to give the reader fair warning, I should note that I will be approaching these narratives with a bit more candour than the tales that I have published previously in "The Strand." In the first place, the intense and rather unusual relationship between Holmes and Miss Adler almost necessitates it, and I am optimistic that my future readers will have left behind some of the more conservative attitudes of the Victorian Age. Secondly,

I have recently been reading the "Confessions" of the French philosopher Jean-Jacques Rousseau, and after being quite taken aback by some of the personal revelations in the opening pages, I found myself warming to the courage and openness of the man. A full recounting of the splendour and tawdriness of the human drama cannot be told with the truth only hinted at or veiled behind various devices, and I feel confident that my friend Sherlock Holmes, who devoted his life to uncovering the truth at any cost, would approve of this course of action. So then, without any further ado, let the truth be told.

(Editor's Note: In the original Sherlock Holmes stories, astute historians noted occasional factual errors and timeline discrepancies, which were invariably put down to the unreliability of Dr. Watson. This tendency did not diminish as the good Doctor entered his later years, but it does not detract in any meaningful way from the pleasure to be had in this long-hidden tale from the annals of Sherlock Holmes.)

Chapter One

Insufficient Funds

London: December 27, 1888.

Should anyone have happened to glance into our rooms at 221B Baker Street on this frigid winter morning, to all appearances I was up, dressed, enjoying a cup of tea, and reading "The Times." However, the reality was that I was in a bit of a fog. It's always the same at this time of year, somewhere between Christmas and New Year's, when I begin to lose track of what day it is and try to ignore a creeping suspicion that I am consuming entirely too much cheese and port.

It always seems like an ideal week to try to get some work done, but instead I find myself reaching for another biscuit, freshening my tea, and sitting in a bit of a stupor as I reminisce about the various women I have known and what I should have done differently. I was in the middle of one of those dark reveries when I heard Holmes' bedroom door open, and I brightened up immediately at the prospect of needling him to see if I could get a rise out of him.

I can't say that I am especially proud of this urge, but I was feeling a bit bored, and if you could have seen Holmes languidly gliding across the room in his embroidered robe, courtesy of the Dalai Lama, he really did make a quite inviting target. And so, as he instinctively made his way towards the teapot…

"There you are, Holmes!" I began. "And about time too! You won't catch me sleeping half the day away. Rise and shine, that's the English way!"

The flickering glance from Holmes in my direction immediately told me that I had made a serious mistake, but since I am long past caring about the approbation of the reading public, I shall not endeavour to spare my blushes. Even as he poured his tea, Holmes calmly replied, "I perceive that you visited Mrs. Nesbitt's fine establishment last night, Watson."

To say that I was stunned would be an understatement. Years of living with Holmes should have prepared me for such an outlandish comment, and I should have had a dazzling riposte ready at hand, but instead all I could manage was, "That's unworthy of you, Holmes! And bloody disgusting! You've been following me through the streets of London!"

"Not at all." Holmes was sipping his tea with the nonchalant air of a man who has just commented that it promises rain in the afternoon.

"You must have! Admit it!" I returned, dimly aware that I wasn't helping my case any, but too outraged to think clearly.

"Nonsense." Holmes was now absorbed in the selection of a piece of shortbread, which had come in the form of a Christmas present from a highly satisfied client in Scotland.

"Then how..." I faltered on, "...not that I'm admitting anything, but..."

Holmes took a seat on the divan, crossed his legs in that damnably insouciant way of his, and cast his eyes towards the ceiling. "A simple matter of elementary deduction. When you went out early in the evening you were, for some reason, in a somewhat peevish frame of mind. The dusting of chalk on your left cuff indicates that you made your way to your club, where you apparently engaged your friend Thurston in a game of billiards, no doubt with the idea of relieving him of a few pounds. The vigour with which you slammed the door upon your return indicated that your plan did not go well—"

"Because Thurston is a bloody cheat!" I interrupted.

"—and then not two minutes later I heard our door open quietly, but with no accompanying footsteps, which indicated that you were carrying your shoes in your hand and didn't wish to be heard going back out," Holmes continued. "The late hour severely limited the number of establishments that you might visit, and now this morning I find you in a calm and relaxed state of mind that can't simply be explained by a good night's sleep. *Quod est demonstratum.*"

Well, that was that—one of the many hazards of living with a deductive genius, which heretofore I haven't seen fit to inflict upon the reading public. The truth is that the number of embarrassingly accurate observations that Holmes made on a regular basis regarding my personal life would be enough to fill several volumes. In this case, the only thing left to do was make an attempt to retreat in good order and save as much face as possible.

Yes, I had lost an uncomfortably large amount of money to Thurston at the table, I had then returned home furious with myself, and immediately upon entering my bedroom realised that sleep would be several hours off until I calmed down. Certainly I could have picked up one of Clark Russell's splendid sea stories or consolidated some of my case notes, but once the thought of a visit to Mrs. Nesbitt's entered my mind, I'm afraid there was no chance of dislodging it.

"I simply needed a drink or two and some decent company to help settle my nerves," I explained to Holmes. "And Mrs. Nesbitt happens to be an excellent conversationalist!"

"I never doubted it for an instant."

Was that a ghost of a smile playing on Holmes' lips? I'm almost certain that it was, but he had artfully turned away from me so I couldn't fully read his expression.

"Yes, well, in the future I will thank you to keep your *quod est* demonstrating to yourself," I returned. I would have gone on further to explain how Thurston has developed the damnable skill of shielding the cue ball with his considerable bulk and surreptitiously adjusting its position an inch or so with his cue, but at that very moment the door to Holmes' bedroom opened and Irene Adler came into the room.

The reader will trust me, I'm sure, when I say that words can't adequately convey her appearance. Not that she was a great beauty, by any means. Out in public, properly attired and coiffed, she was largely indistinguishable from any other fashionable woman—just another face in the crowd as it were. But here in our rooms, clad only in the silk Japanese robe she favoured, with her hair in some degree of dishabille, and her dark, intelligent eyes flashing at Holmes, she was nothing less than breathtaking. As was her custom, she sauntered towards Holmes and sat down on his lap.

"Is that tea?" she asked.

"Indeed it is, my sweet!" Holmes returned. "Courtesy of the estimable Dr. Watson."

Miss Adler took a small sip and then favoured me with a smile, "Mmm...delicious."

"As always," Holmes answered. "Our Watson is something of a tea savant."

Pleased as I was to hear this small praise, when Miss Adler reached for a piece of Holmes' shortbread, her robe slipped slightly, revealing a generous expanse of thigh, and I'm afraid my Victorian training was as reflexive as it was instantaneous.

"Really, Miss Adler!" I expostulated. "A little decency, please!"

"Oh, for Heaven's sake! You're a doctor! Surely you've seen a woman's leg before."

"Well, of course I have!" I answered. "But—"

"Come now, my dear," Holmes interjected. "A little decorum for the good doctor's sake. He had quite enough excitement last night at Mrs. Nesbitt's."

"Did he?" Miss Adler's eyebrows arched up as she turned to me. "Well, I hope you closed your eyes and thought of England."

Holmes found this most amusing, and Miss Adler was delighted to have amused him, but for me, it was a bit much. I was still on edge regarding Thurston's cheating, and Holmes' all-too-accurate deduction had unsettled me even further, so I put my teacup down with a clatter, stood up, and prepared to let them both have a piece of my mind. "Right. Now listen to me, you two! I know how much you're both in love with your own cleverness, but I've been meaning to have a word—"

"This can't be good," said Miss Adler.

"It never is," agreed Holmes.

"—regarding the state of affairs in this household!"

Holmes leaned closer to Miss Adler, "He's all wound up on tea."

"Shh. He's trying to say something," replied Miss Adler as she extricated herself from Holmes' lap in search of more tea and a scone.

So it was that I now found myself in the position of addressing an unpleasant topic that I had been trying to avoid for several weeks. "Thank you. Yes, I am trying to say something. Now then, I am well aware of just how stupid I am. I get daily reminders from the both of you about how mind-numbingly slow and thick I must be because I can't solve

11

murders based on the depth to which the parsley has sunk into the butter on a hot summer day. However, despite my vast and apparently unending ignorance, allow me to point out that I am the only one here actually making money."

You could have heard a pin drop. For Holmes and Miss Adler, the subject of finances ranked somewhere in interest between yearly rainfall in the Amazon and 12th-century popes. They both looked at me in consternation.

"What? No! That can't be true!" Holmes turned to Miss Adler for support. "Is that true?"

"It might be," she conceded.

Emboldened by their uncertainty, I turned to the harsh world of irrefutable facts. "I get paid fifty pounds for every story of yours I write up in 'The Strand Magazine,'" I told Holmes. "When was the last time you got paid for a case?"

"Well…" Holmes hesitated, then uttered the words I knew were coming next. "The work is its own reward!"

"No, it isn't! Money is its own reward! Pounds, sovereigns, half crowns. A bloody farthing, for God's sake! I'm the only one paying the bills!"

But just as Holmes had the decency to look a bit abashed, Miss Adler sailed to his rescue, declaring, "But as you said, it's our cases that you write up. We're the ones giving you material."

"Excellent point, my dear!"

"I thought so," Miss Adler replied as she and Holmes proceeded to clink their teacups together, quite pleased with themselves. However, I had been preparing for this particular discussion for some time now, and so I brought out my trusty notebook.

"Oh really? You provide the material? Let's just go over your last few cases, shall we?" Opening the notebook, I began to read. "Here we are...last Thursday, Mrs. Pickford of 73 Govan Street lost her cat, Mr. Jingles. You retrieved the cat from a dustbin where it had fallen asleep. You followed up this triumph when Mr. Hainsely of 14 Whiston Road reported his wife missing and suspected murdered. Miss Adler found her in the alley behind her usual pub in a drunken stupor and brought her home. And just yesterday, Lady Claybourne's supposedly stolen emerald necklace was found in the pocket of her own nightgown, where she had forgotten she put it because she's getting a bit senile."

"Ah, but we did find it!" responded Holmes. "You know our methods, Watson. When you eliminate the impossible, whatever remains, however improbable, must be the truth."

"And when you eliminate any source of income, what remains is getting thrown out into the street because you can't pay the bloody rent! I can't write up any of those cases as a new adventure."

"Why not?" enquired Miss Adler.

"Seriously? You think people want to sit down and read 'The Adventure of the Sleeping Pussycat' or 'The Adventure of the Not Actually Stolen Jewellery?' No! No, they don't! I may not know much, but I do know the kinds of stories the reading public enjoys! We need something with an edge! Something foreign, dangerous, a master criminal—"

"Like Professor Moriarty?" offered Holmes.

"Exactly!" I agreed. "Professor Moriarty! The Napoleon of Crime! Sitting like a giant spider at the centre of London's underworld, plotting and scheming the most bizarre and outlandish crimes imaginable. That's precisely what we need! Except someone in this room, and I'm not pointing fingers, someone in this room threw him off a waterfall!"

"That was you, sweetheart," said Miss Adler.

"It seemed like a good idea at the time," replied Holmes.

"Well, it wasn't!" I continued. "Moriarty gave you two a challenge! He gave you something to do, and that gave me something to write about. I'm not saying that psychopathic criminals don't have their downside, but they're a damned sight more interesting than sleeping pussycats!"

And here, I was foolishly optimistic enough to think that with my point made, Holmes and Miss Adler would begin discussing sensible and pragmatic steps to address my concerns regarding our finances. But no. Miss Adler had one more salvo to offer, one that had raised its ugly head a number of times since she had moved in with us.

"Well then," she began, "I have the perfect suggestion. If you want something a bit more exciting, why not a story that's a full and honest description of our relationship and the way we work?"

I groaned inwardly. "We've gone over this..."

Like Holmes, Miss Adler was sometimes a little too in love with her own brilliance, and so on she rattled as she made her way to Holmes' desk. Some time ago, Holmes had flattered me by placing a copy of "The Strand" containing the story "A Scandal in Bohemia" in a frame and placing it on his desk. He never mentioned it to me or alluded to it, but I knew it was his way of thanking me for writing the story that had resulted in his worldwide fame.

"I only appear under my real name in 'A Scandal in Bohemia'..." Miss Adler went on, removing the magazine from its frame and leafing through it. "Here we are! 'To Sherlock Holmes she is always *the* woman. I have seldom heard him mention her under any other name. In his eyes she eclipses and predominates the whole of her sex...there was but one woman to him, and that woman was the late Irene Adler, of dubious and questionable memory.' Why did you have to kill me?"

"Because that's the way stories work. Sherlock Holmes is the hero, and heroes don't have lovers or wives or women of any sort in their lives."

"Why not?"

"Because they get in the way of being heroic!" This seemed perfectly obvious to me and should have been perfectly obvious to anyone with a passing acquaintance of the past two thousand years of Western Civilisation history and literature, but like a bulldog with a bone, Miss Adler simply wouldn't let it go.

"What about Samson and Delilah?"

"She betrayed him to the Philistines, and they tore his eyes out."

"Jason and Medea?"

"She gets mad at him, so she kills their children."

"Tom Jones and his beloved Sophia?"

This was getting slightly ridiculous, so I determined to put an end to it, taking the magazine from her and putting it back in its frame. "The novel ends once they get married because he's not a hero anymore! Look, it's quite simple, married men are not heroes! Not now, not ever! They're plain, dull, spineless husbands devoted to providing for their wives and children. No more adventures, no more conquests, just a steady, boring walk straight into the grave!"

By now, the tea had well and truly kicked in, so while Miss Adler may have been frustrated on one front, she quickly found another subject for her ire.

"And what do you mean, 'of dubious and questionable memory?' Why am I dubious and questionable?"

"You two only met because you were blackmailing the King of Bohemia!"

"Because he was a complete and utter bastard."

"That may well be, but—"

At long last Holmes, who had been enjoying this exchange just a little too much, deigned to join the discussion. Standing up, he moved towards Miss Adler. "I'm afraid Watson's right, my dear. You are an irredeemably wicked specimen of the female species."

Miss Adler turned to Holmes, raised an eyebrow, and the palpable energy between them was electric. Knowing full well where this was going, I stepped between them. "All right, stop that! Just stop it! Both of you. I'll admit, I thought it was rather charming to see the two of you smitten with one another, and yes, your respective intellectual talents certainly complement one another wonderfully, but I didn't expect..."

"Me to move in?" Miss Adler was talking to me, but her eyes were still locked on Holmes.

"Quite. This is, need I remind you, Victorian England. It's simply not done. So, the only way for me to explain your presence here is for you to be Mrs. Hudson, the devoted housekeeper of Sherlock Holmes."

And here, should the reader require it, I offer a wholehearted apology for this final ruse that I was forced to inflict upon the unsuspecting followers of Sherlock Holmes. Miss Adler clearly lived at 221B, but just as clearly she was not married to Sherlock Holmes or me. Should this come to light, I'm afraid the general public reaction would have been one of universal condemnation. The idea of a respectable single man and a single woman living together because they happened to enjoy one another's company was simply beyond the pale, and if the gutter press got hold of the story, they would have declared it a national scandal. Holmes' name would have been dragged through the mud from one end of the country to the other, the Church of England would have weighed in with its usual pious hypocrisy, and politicians with more mistresses than children would have happily jumped on the bandwagon as well. I don't think it's too much to surmise that Holmes and Miss Adler would have been hounded out of the country by the press and the mob.

Mind you, when Miss Adler had first moved in, I took it for granted that their nuptials would not be far off, and even went to the trouble of making sure that my best suit still fit me. Weeks passed, then months, and when I finally enquired as to whether or not they had a date when the wedding bells would ring, they both looked at me as if I were a madman. I may as well have asked if they had a date for travelling to Italy to jump into the Stromboli volcano.

I therefore attempted to accommodate myself to our new living arrangements with patience and good grace, and I must say, witnessing Holmes and Miss Adler at close quarters, it was abundantly clear that their relationship would not be improved in any way by a slip of paper indicating religious and governmental approval.

However, outside of 221B, I was well aware that the idea of Holmes and Miss Adler being in love and living together, but not bothering to get married would surely signal the end of the British Empire. I also knew very well that I couldn't present Holmes and Miss Adler as some kind of detecting duo, for no one would ever believe it. Still, I had to somehow account for her presence at 221B Baker Street and yet be able to continue to recount the remarkable exploits of Sherlock Holmes in "The

Strand Magazine" for the benefit of the British reading public and, I might add, our bank account. Searching for some kind of answer to this dilemma caused me more than one sleepless night before I landed on the easiest and most obvious solution—in the stories Miss Adler would be our housekeeper!

Accordingly, in my first short story I simply plucked "Mrs. Turner" out of thin air as the name of our "housekeeper," but by the time I came to write "The Adventure of the Blue Carbuncle," I decided that I wanted her name to subtly suggest a connection to Holmes, and I didn't have to look far for a solution. When Holmes and I had first taken rooms together, our landlady had been a middle-aged woman by the name of Mrs. Hudson, who lived on the premises. However, she was of a somewhat inquisitive disposition, and after walking in on Holmes conducting a chemical experiment on two human kidneys, she had speedily relocated to her sister's home in Shoreditch. It dawned on me that "Mrs. Hudson" was indeed the perfect pseudonym for Miss Adler, and so I simply made the change with no explanation.

This subsequently led to considerable comment and analysis by devoted admirers of Holmes over the years. Had I misremembered her name? Were there two housekeepers? And on and on and on. I remember with some fondness the moment when Holmes was upbraiding me for my lack of creativity in the naming of "Mrs. Hudson" as he and Miss Adler lounged about while I worked on the text of "The Naval Treaty." For all of his admirable and sterling qualities, Holmes was not above a bit of petty sniping when he was bored.

On this particular occasion, Miss Adler was immersed in Gibbon's "The Decline and Fall of the Roman Empire," and Holmes had already spent a good few minutes staring out the window and lamenting the lack of creativity of London's criminal class. When he strolled over to the desk where I was working and peered over my shoulder, I knew there was trouble coming as he read the text.

"If I might venture a bit of literary criticism, Watson, I must say that your choice of the name 'Mrs. Hudson' for Irene wasn't particularly inspired. Why not something with a bit more panache?"

Without even looking up from her book, Miss Adler instantly commented, "That's Watson's little cipher, my dear. Hudson, six letters, starts with the letter 'H.' Holmes, six letters, starts with the letter..." Miss Adler kindly left the rest of her sentence hanging, allowing our resident deductive genius to fill in the blank.

"Oh, I see! That's rather clever, actually. Well done, old boy!"

"Thank you," I returned. "I am proud of that particular authorial flourish, now that you mention it, although I'm sure most readers won't notice."

"Well, most readers don't have Irene's peculiar sensitivity insofar as names and language are concerned. In fact, Irene has quite a number of, shall we say, peculiarly sensitive areas, don't you, my dear?" Miss Adler closed her book firmly to fix Holmes with a stare.

"Was that absolutely necessary?"

"I'm afraid so, my sweet. I'm absolutely bored out of my mind."

Miss Adler turned to me, "I'm sorry you had to hear that, Dr. Watson."

"No, not at all," I waved off her concern. "I've heard worse."

"I'm well aware of that, and I do thank you for your discretion in your stories."

Being an American, Miss Adler and I did have differences of opinion on a great number of topics; for example, Great Britain's colonial activities, the whole notion of a royal family, and the relative merits of cricket as opposed to baseball. However, the one thing that we did share in common was living with Sherlock Holmes. Given that, we had become allies to one another whenever Holmes' conversation or behaviour stretched the bounds of decency and decorum.

Over time, I had come to not only respect, but admire the facility with which she could command and redirect Holmes' attention. This was especially true whenever I was working on a new story. Gradually, I came to realise that as I agonised over just the right word or phrase, that Holmes had been quietly spirited out of the room by Miss Adler so that I might work in peace.

Ah, but I digress from the case at hand. In the company of clients, Miss Adler took on the role of Mrs. Hudson with good grace and humour, even giving her a Cockney accent from time to time to amuse herself. At other times, she chafed under the alias that I had assigned her, and this morning, I am sorry to say, was one of those times.

Chapter Two
First Impressions

Miss Adler had a habit of pacing when she was thinking or agitated, and as she walked back and forth, I braced myself for the inevitable.

"I know that referring to me as Mrs. Hudson is a convenient device," she began, "but I think it's high time that we did something with the very dull, boring, and dreary Mrs. Hudson."

"What are you thinking, my dear?" Holmes encouraged her.

"Mrs. Hudson should die. Violently. She should be killed off by a pygmy or a ravenous school of piranhas. Then the beautiful and marvellously insightful Irene Adler miraculously comes back to life and moves in with Sherlock Holmes, whereupon they form a detecting team based on their mutual brilliance and lust for one another."

She turned her eyes on Holmes, who smiled. "I must say I like the sound of that."

All I could do was shake my head. "Do you two even read the stories I write? Sherlock Holmes is a bachelor! An emotionless calculating machine. Expert boxer, single-stick player, and swordsman—"

Miss Adler burst into laughter. "Swordsman?"

Ignoring her, I shouldered on, "—plays the violin passably well and smokes a pipe. Knowledge of art, philosophy, and politics—feeble. Knowledge of chemistry and sensational literature—profound. Oh, and one more tiny detail. He doesn't like women."

"Then who was that in bed with me last night?"

Holmes held his hand up and waved.

"For God's sake," I continued, "I can't write that you two are anything but a confirmed bachelor and his plain and dutiful housekeeper."

"Why do I have to be plain?"

"What am I supposed to say? 'Into the room stepped our housekeeper, Mrs. Hudson, her exquisite feminine form barely concealed by her silk robe...'"

"I like that much better."

"Hear, hear!" chimed in Holmes. "He does have a way with words."

"You two aren't even bloody married!" I regretted those words the moment I uttered them, but it was too late. Miss Adler looked at me as if I had just suggested that a roasted Scottish terrier would be a tasty supper.

"Of course we're not married! Why should we sanction and participate in a patriarchal society that systematically deprives women of their most basic rights?"

And with that, she was off on one of her pet subjects. Not that I didn't agree with her wholeheartedly, but it was still early in the day, and my head was beginning to hurt, so I made my way to the tantalus and poured myself some brandy. Behind me, Miss Adler was picking up steam.

"We can't vote, can't own property...oh, no. We're supposed to be the Angel of the House, who quivers in excitement at the idea of a bargain at the shops or a freshly scrubbed kitchen floor, our sole focus the happiness and contentment of the man who has been gracious enough to take us in and to provide our poor, simple souls with all that we need simply by being in his presence."

I drained my glass, shook my head, and poured another. "It's pointless. I try to explain things, but I may as well be speaking Swahili."

"Irene speaks Swahili. Don't you, dear?"

"*Kidogo tu.*"

I turned back towards them, and they resembled nothing less than two puppies quite delighted that they have chewed a new pair of boots to pieces. With my hopes of any kind of productive discourse rapidly ebbing, I slowly made my way to the window. "I'm going to try this one last time. We need money. I thought I could take a few quid off Thurston at billiards last night, but that didn't go very well. London is an expensive city and these rooms are not cheap. Tea, scones, tobacco, cocaine...it adds up."

"All right, then," reasoned Holmes, "we'll have to give up scones."

"Speak for yourself," replied Miss Adler, helping herself to another scone.

Holmes carried on, "So, what you're saying is, we need a case. The more bizarre and inexplicable, the better. Something colourful and mystifying, preferably with a dash of foreign intrigue, and behind it all a shadowy, malevolent intelligence. Something like—"

"—like this fellow coming down the street."

I don't normally interrupt Holmes when he's speaking, but the individual I had just observed walking down Baker Street was very remarkable indeed. Judging by his shabby attire, he was clearly not a wealthy man, and he carried a travelling case and some sort of package beneath his arm. He was absolutely indifferent to any passersby, apparently in a world of his own, bumping into both men and women as he swiveled his head this way and that, and in the process revealing a bloody bandage wrapped around his head.

Any more immediate details were impossible to observe as I felt myself being pulled back from the window by Holmes and Miss Adler, who stared down at the street intently, then began batting deductions back and forth like a shuttlecock, as was their habit.

"He's carrying a travelling case and looking at house numbers, which means he's a stranger to the area."

"Left-handed."

"Not English."

"But northern European heritage."

"True, but most recently residing in a much warmer climate."

I hadn't the faintest doubt that all of these observations were quite accurate, but they were all utterly irrelevant as far as I was concerned. My mind was consumed with one and only one thought—please be a client. So when our bell rang, my relief and elation fairly leapt out of me. "Yes! A client! It's a client!"

After much thought and discussion it had been decided that retrieving clients from our doorstep was "Mrs. Hudson's" province, and so Miss Adler duly headed for the door, but I was able to head her off before she got too far in her revealing silk robe. "Not like that! Put your...something more decent, please!"

"Why?" Miss Adler was all feigned innocence.

"So it doesn't look like we live in an Oriental brothel, that's why!"

"Forgive him, my dear," said Holmes. "He's English."

"Obviously," remarked Miss Adler as she headed back to the bedroom to change. Casting a reproving look at Holmes, I made my way to the window and opened it, anxious to make certain that our potential client didn't wander off.

"I say! Hello there! Up here! Yes, hello! Mrs. Hudson will be down straightaway. She's coming! Don't go anywhere!"

As our visitor glanced upwards, I caught sight of his striking blue eyes, but then Miss Adler was bustling across the room, tying the sash of a plain, full-length robe, and getting into her Mrs. Hudson character with a full-blown Cockney accent.

"I'll just let the bloke in then, shall I, guv?"

"Please don't do that." Mindful of our guest's Continental origins, I didn't want "Mrs. Hudson" scaring him off with an incomprehensible accent.

"Do what, guv'nor? Go down the apples and pears?"

"Oh God…"

However, this was a game that Holmes particularly enjoyed; that is, translating "Mrs. Hudson's" Cockney gibberish as fast as she could spew it out.

"The stairs!"

"Earn some bees and honey for the Duke of Kent?"

"Hold on, I know this one…earn some money for the rent!"

This, I knew, could go on and on, so I had to intercede. "Just go let the poor bastard in before he bleeds to death on our front steps."

With that, Miss Adler moved towards the door heading downstairs, but she had one last bit of Cockney left in her, which she directed at Holmes, "Your friend's a bit of a Hampton Wick."

As she disappeared down the stairs, I turned to Holmes, who helpfully began to explain, "That means you're a—"

"I know what it bloody well means!"

"Oh, come now. She's just having a bit of fun. And it's part of her Mrs. Hudson character."

"Speaking of which..."

For all of his intellect, Holmes was often unmindful of the importance of appearance. In concert with my illustrator, Sidney Paget, in the stories we had worked very hard to build up in the public mind a certain picture of the great detective, both indoors and out. Outside, of course, Holmes was instantly identifiable by his iconic deerstalker, which he wore for our visits to the countryside. Indoors was a bit more difficult, and I felt it required both props and particular poses, so even as I heard the downstairs door opening, I was shepherding Holmes into position.

"Sit over here in the armchair...legs crossed...for God's sake we've done this before, yes? Now, fingers steepled together like you're thinking about something of massive importance..."

"Such as?"

"It doesn't matter! It's important! Massively important!"

"Well, it would be a bit easier if you could give me some kind of description. What sort of case am I working on?"

"It's a murder! It's a horrible, violent, ghastly murder."

"I see. And who has been murdered?"

"It doesn't matter!"

"It does to me."

"It's a Duke! A very important Duke sort of person. With a ridiculously large estate because one of his ancestors helped Charles I kidnap a village girl for nefarious purposes."

"Excellent. And who are the suspects?"

"Holmes, please..."

"We must have suspects, Watson."

"Very well. The suspects are as follows: the Duke's gardener, Maurice Wileman, who has a drinking problem and a violent attachment to his petunias, which the Duke has a habit of stepping on; his valet, Charles Dixon, who has been selling the Duke's books to a pawnbroker to finance his gambling habit; his eldest son James, who is fed up waiting to become a Duke; and his wife Constance, who has loathed him from the day they got married and wishes to flee to Brazil with her lover, Rodrigo, a one-legged horse-trainer prone to occasional bouts of dropsy."

"Excellent, Watson! You really do have a rare facility for storytelling. You should take it up seriously at some point."

Resisting the urge to cuff Holmes about the ear, I stepped back to survey him. With his legs crossed and fingers steepled together, he was clearly rounding into shape, but all the same, there was something missing.

"Your pipe! Where's your pipe?" It was the most astonishing thing that Holmes must have had at least half a dozen pipes, but they all went missing at the very moment we needed one. Footsteps could now be heard ascending the stairs as I finally spotted Holmes' briar peeking out from beneath some papers on the mantelpiece.

"There we are!" I put the pipe in Holmes' mouth and then adjusted his robe. "Excellent! You look like a proper consulting detective now."

"You're too kind. Shouldn't you assume your official position?"

"Yes, of course!"

A moment later I was on the divan, apparently completely engrossed in "The Times" as the door opened and Miss Adler ushered our somewhat peculiar visitor into the room. Seen at close quarters, his clothing was even more disreputable and

27

unkempt than it had appeared at first glance, consisting of a green overcoat, a blue hat with some kind of black fur at the front, worn shoes, and pants that were cuffed at the bottom. His small travelling case was spattered with paint, which made me suspect that the canvas-wrapped item beneath his arm might be a painting of some kind.

Most striking of all, of course, was the bloody bandage wrapped around his head, with the dark hue of the blood indicating that it had not been changed in some time. Taking into consideration all of these features, my first thought was that he scarcely appeared to be the sort of client likely to improve our bank statement to any undue extent. Still, protocol is protocol, and Holmes and I both stood to greet our visitor as he looked about in a distracted, almost hunted fashion.

"Ah, do come in! I am Sherlock Holmes and this is my colleague, Dr. Watson. Whom do we have the pleasure of addressing?"

Our visitor's pale blue eyes searched ours for a moment, looking for who knows what, until he muttered in a guttural Dutch accent, "My name is Vincent. Van Gogh."

Bearing in mind my earlier promise to be completely candid with my readers, I am afraid that my subsequent actions did not do me any particular credit. I pulled out my handkerchief and held it towards Van Gogh. "You poor fellow. Here, take my handkerchief."

Our visitor gazed at the handkerchief, then back at me, utterly baffled. To my alarm, I saw that both Holmes and Miss Adler were staring at me in some confusion as well.

"That's his name," offered Holmes.

"What's his name?"

Holmes made a valiant effort to replicate the sounds that had just emerged from our visitor. "Van Gogh. That's his name."

"No, it isn't." I'd had just about enough of indulging Holmes and his peculiar sense of humour. "He's got some phlegm in his throat...some kind of mucus. You might be coming down with something, Mr...?"

Again came that horrid noise from our visitor, which I can only describe as being akin to hearing an asthmatic badger being strangled. This immediately posed a difficulty for me, because I do like to be formal and professional with our clients, but knew with absolute certainty that I would never be able to make that dry, gargling sound come out of my mouth.

"Good Lord..." I reached for the back of the divan to steady myself, even as I could see Miss Adler fighting back laughter. Holmes, professional as ever, carried on as if nothing out of the ordinary had just happened. "Pray let us have your coat and hat and take a seat, Mr. Van Gogh. Mrs. Hudson, would you be so kind as to fetch our guest a cup of tea? For I perceive that his journey has been both long and arduous."

"A bit o' Rosy Lee? No trouble, no trouble. He's in a bit of two and eight, he is."

Van Gogh put his travelling case and wrapped package down near the fireplace, then removed his hat and coat to reveal clothing spattered with paint and paintbrushes protruding from his jacket pocket. Holmes guided Van Gogh to the divan and they both sat down as I took Van Gogh's hat and coat to the coat stand and Miss Adler poured a cup of tea.

Holmes smiled pleasantly at our guest, endeavouring to put him at ease. "Yes, as Mrs. Hudson so eloquently put it, you do seem to be in something of a state, Mr. Van Gogh."

"To put it mildly."

In situations like this, I often try to put myself into Holmes' shoes and see the world through his eyes. Despite his ingratiating and casual demeanour, I knew very well that Holmes was cataloguing our visitor from head to foot. Every article of clothing, every gesture and reaction would be assessed and measured as Holmes built up a complete history of the man ranging from his childhood to what he might have eaten for breakfast. I never flattered myself by thinking that I could even remotely approach the accuracy of Holmes' observations and deductions, but yes, it was abundantly clear that our visitor was in a state of severe emotional distress.

His pale blue eyes rarely landed on anything for more than a moment, and he rubbed his paint-stained hands together incessantly. With his gaunt face and lines of worry tracking across his forehead, I would have ventured that he was nearing fifty years of age, but when I was subsequently inspired to look up his day of birth many years after the case, I was shocked to learn that the man sitting before me was a mere thirty-five years old.

At length, Miss Adler arrived with a cup of tea and handed it to Van Gogh. "There we are. Get that down your billy goat and you'll be right as dodgers."

As Van Gogh looked around in mystification, I took pity on the man. "Just enjoy your tea, Mr...do you mind if I call you Vincent? Vince? Vinny, perhaps?"

"Anything is fine." In two gulps he had drained his cup, and I wondered when was the last time he had had anything to eat or drink. The same thought clearly struck Holmes as well.

"More tea for our guest, Mrs. Hudson. And perhaps a scone or two."

"Yes, of course," replied Miss Adler, taking Van Gogh's cup to refill it. "He might enjoy some shortbread as well, if you don't mind my saying so."

"Capital idea!" agreed Holmes, before turning his attention back to Van Gogh. "Now then, Mr. Van Gogh, how may we be of service to you?"

Van Gogh swallowed hard and seemed to be on the verge of tears. "I scarcely know where to begin. These past four days have been a nightmare. I have suffered a great many tragedies and indignities over the years, but now I fear that my life is beyond repair."

"You have incurred a wound, I see. Were you attacked?"

"No, I..." Van Gogh broke off in some distress as Miss Adler returned with more tea and a plate heaped with scones and shortbread. Helping himself to a piece of shortbread, Van Gogh took a small bite, the crumbs tumbling from his lips, and I observed that his hand was trembling. Taking a sip of tea, he gathered himself and continued. "The wound is self-inflicted, I fear."

"Indeed? Dr. Watson, would you mind...?"

Glad of something to do, I approached Van Gogh. "May I examine your wound?"

As I reached for the bandage, Van Gogh covered his ear and shied away, clearly apprehensive. It was an awkward moment, until Miss Adler broke the silence.

"Cor, blimey, leave off, will you? The poor bloke's humiliated enough as it is! Mark my words, there's a woman at the bottom of this."

The effect of Miss Adler's words on Van Gogh was electric. He shot to his feet, as if being pulled up by strings held by an invisible puppet master.

"How could you possibly know that?"

"I'm psychic. I can read your mind clear across the room, I can."

Van Gogh's eyes went wide. "Can you really?"

"No, no. Calm yourself, Mr. Van Gogh," soothed Holmes. "Mrs. Hudson will have her little jokes. She's not psychic. She's just a very good guesser. Please take your seat. You're among friends here. Dr. Watson, your professional opinion, please."

With Van Gogh retaking his seat, I lifted up his bandage to peer beneath it. What I saw was not a pretty sight, although I had certainly seen worse on the battlefields of Afghanistan. Still, if what Van Gogh said was true about the origin of the wound, it was obvious that he had effectively mutilated himself for life. But why? What moment of madness could possibly have precipitated such an act? Carefully replacing the bandage, I turned to Holmes, "He appears to have completely severed the lower portion of his ear with an extremely sharp instrument of some kind."

"Ya," offered Van Gogh, "with my razor."

Holmes looked closely at Van Gogh. "And you did this to yourself, you say?"

Van Gogh managed a nod, then dropped his head into his hands as his body shook with sobs. I glanced at Holmes for some kind of direction, but he was clearly just as much at sea as I was. A moment later, I felt Miss Adler at my shoulder.

"If I might make a deduction, I think Dutch boy needs something a bit stronger than tea, Dr. Watson."

"What? Oh, yes, of course! What's your pleasure, Vince? Brandy? Cognac?"

Van Gogh looked up at me. "Have you any absinthe?"

"Absinthe? No, can't say that we do. Fresh out, I'm afraid."

"Put absinthe on your shopping list, Mrs. Hudson," said Holmes.

"Will do! Can never have enough addictive psychoactive drugs around here, can we?"

Van Gogh was taking deep breaths and slowly regaining his composure. "Then some brandy please."

As I moved to pour a snifter of brandy for our guest, Miss Adler somehow produced a feather duster out of thin air and proceeded to dust anything and everything in her vicinity, but with her attention fully focused on Van Gogh. Holmes waited patiently until I had delivered the brandy into Van Gogh's hands, then leaned back in his chair. "Now then, would you care to recount the series of events that led to your self-mutilation?"

"Very well. It all began with...Paul."

"Paul?"

"Gauguin." Van Gogh took a gulp of brandy. "I would like to say that he is a colleague, but perhaps he would deny that word. Better perhaps, to say that I am a great admirer of his. Like me, he is a painter, but Gauguin is an exceptional artist. I was speaking about him to a friend of mine, and she suggested that I invite Paul to the south of France to stay with me in the town of Arles, so that we might paint together. I thought it was a wonderful idea, and so I wrote to him about starting a small artists' colony."

I was busy taking notes as Van Gogh told his tale, but out of the corner of my eye, I noticed Miss Adler waving her duster in the air. "Excuse me interrupting, but did you mention absinthe a bit ago? My old man used to love the absinthe. The Green Fairy, he called it. Here's the thing though. Drink enough, and it drives you barking mad it does."

Van Gogh nodded. "I am aware of absinthe's reputation, and ya, I have moments when I am twisted with joy or madness or prophecy, like a Greek oracle. In such a state, I will confess that I have been seized by the most uncontrollable urges."

"As the bandage around your head would indicate," Holmes interjected. "Do go on with your story. You and Mr. Gauguin took up residence together."

"Ya. I do not know if you are familiar with the town of Arles, Mr. Holmes, but it is a most wonderful place situated in Provence, in the south of France. It is on the Rhône River, just north of the Mediterranean Sea, and the light there is the most unique that I have found in all the world. Colours glow. The sky, the fields, the water. Even the air shimmers as you gaze upon it. If you will let your senses and not your mind guide you, it is magical beyond belief, and it is where I have finally found myself as an artist.

"When Paul arrived, he was delighted to find himself in such a beautiful place. He was inspired, just as I was inspired, and at first, things were going well between us. We were both working during the day and then frequenting the cafés at night. But at length, certain tensions began to grow."

A thought occurred to me. "Would those tensions be due to the woman Mrs. Hudson mentioned?"

Van Gogh nodded and in an instant Miss Adler was sitting at his side, and with her kind smile and shining eyes, she was every bit the kind of woman to whom you would instantly confess the darkest secrets of your soul, which was precisely what she had in mind.

Chapter Three
Van Gogh's Muse

Miss Adler put her hand gently on Van Gogh's arm and stared not so much into his eyes, but his very soul. "Are you in love with 'er?" she began. "Is she beautiful? She must be. Is she kind? Intelligent? Tell us all about 'er."

"Tell you about Rachel?"

"Is that 'er name? What a beautiful name! Wouldn't you agree, Mr. Holmes?"

"Indeed I would," nodded Holmes. "And you met her in Arles?"

Van Gogh looked from side to side at the pleasant expressions of Holmes and Miss Adler. To all intents and purposes he could have been sitting with his two oldest friends in the world. I, of course, knew better. Having sized up the mental and emotional state of Mr. Van Gogh, both Holmes and Miss Adler had adopted the demeanour they felt was best suited to get the most information out of him.

Indeed, as I took in this particular tableau, I was irresistibly reminded of nothing less than a small rabbit peacefully going about its business in an open field, being watched with rapt attention by two nearby hawks.

"Rachel..." Van Gogh began, "...was dropped from heaven by God Himself. You will think me a fool for saying so, but that is the truth. I had been in Arles on my own for perhaps a month, and after a long day painting in the fields had retired to a café for a drink and simple meal. I was not in the best state of mind, for my money was running low and I was not happy with my work. The next day promised more of the same, and I felt that I simply could not go on, could not bear the emptiness and the sadness of my life.

"And so there I was, alone, tired, my home in Holland perhaps a thousand kilometres away, and this angel simply appeared out of nowhere and sat across from me. Not a word did she say…not a word. She simply looked at me, and for the first time in my life I felt known. Somehow, I knew that she had seen my pain, seen my suffering, and she had descended from the skies to give me a reason to live. And from that day forward everything changed. I saw the world as I had never seen it before, and I was finally able to paint the beauty I could now see."

"Ah, I begin to understand," remarked Holmes.

"Do you?" asked Van Gogh.

"Well, by all means correct me if I'm wrong," continued Holmes, "but logic dictates that this angel of a woman would have your best interests at heart, yes?"

"Ya! Of course!" agreed Van Gogh.

"So then, seeing your loneliness and dissatisfaction with your work, not only did she seek to inspire you by her sheer presence, she was no doubt the woman who suggested that you invite Paul Gauguin to reside with you in Arles."

"Ya!" This was all simple enough for me to follow, but Van Gogh stared at Holmes as if he was in the presence of some kind of wizard.

"Oh, what a luv!" enthused Miss Adler. "She 'ad your best interests at 'eart, she did."

"Unlike Paul Gauguin, as it turned out," added Holmes.

Van Gogh nodded. "I first met Paul in Paris. I had heard rumours about him, as one hears rumours about all artists, but I had ignored them. Artists, I am sorry to say, can be a petty, envious group of people, and I shudder to think of the stories that are told about me in the Parisian cafés. That was just one more reason that I left Paris, to get away from the jealousy and gossip and to simply paint. But then, practically from the moment he arrived, Paul had eyes for Rachel. How could he not? She was pleasant to him, and kind. At first, knowing of my infatuation with her, he tried to pretend his indifference. But that was a charade that did not last long.

"He began to try to seduce her, began giving her his paintings, much as I had done, but she resisted his charms. Or at least, I believe she did. Perhaps I was seeing only what I wanted to see. Then, it became clear that he was becoming more familiar with her. I could see it in every word, every gesture. He denied it, of course, but by then I could see through his lies. Ultimately, we had words...harsh words. Our final argument spilled out into the street. Paul said that he loved her more than me and that he would paint for her the greatest painting of his life and that she would never look at me again."

At this, Van Gogh got to his feet, in a haze of pain even at the memory. "I didn't know what to do. I was in a rage of fear and anguish. He is the better painter...more handsome...more refined in his manners. But he does not love as I do! He does not know what I know—that there is nothing more purely artistic than to love! So when I reached into my pocket and felt a razor, I knew in an instant that I could give her a gift surpassing anything he could compose on a canvas. I would give her a piece of myself..."

And then, as we looked on in fascination, Van Gogh lifted his left hand to where the lobe of his left ear would have been. With an imaginary razor in his right hand, he sliced through his ear, back to front.

Holmes watched this performance closely, scarcely even blinking. "A striking tale, Mr. Van Gogh. May I see your wound?"

"But Dr. Watson has already—"

"Please."

"If you must."

Holmes retrieved his magnifying lens and approached Van Gogh, eyeing him from head to foot. He felt the fabric of Van Gogh's lapel, sniffed at a paint stain or two, then knelt down to inspect Van Gogh's shoes. Standing up again, he lifted up Van Gogh's bandage and peered beneath it with his lens, then stepped back a pace or two to regard Van Gogh at full length.

"Fascinating."

"What is it, Holmes?" I asked. "I saw nothing remarkable."

"No? Then you saw but failed to observe. Yours is a very unique and compelling story, Mr. Van Gogh..." Here Holmes paused, and seemed to be choosing his next words very carefully, "...and I don't doubt the whole experience was devastating for you."

Van Gogh nodded his agreement. "And the most devastating thing of all is what has brought me here. You are the only man in Europe who can help me, Mr. Holmes, which is why I spent my very last franc to make the journey to London."

As intrigued as I had been by Van Gogh's strange tale and Holmes' examination, this jolted me back to reality. "I'm sorry, what was that? You spent what?"

"My last franc to make the trip here."

"You mean to say that you have no money?"

"No. I am a poor artist, Dr. Watson."

"But you can raise some, surely? How much do your paintings typically sell for?"

Van Gogh cast his eyes upon the ground. "I regret to say that I have yet to sell a single painting."

As I looked at Holmes, absolutely speechless, Miss Adler broke the awkward silence.

"Well, not to worry. The art business is a tough nut to crack, eh? You sell one or two pieces and they'll be flying off the shelves like hotcakes, they will. You just need to get yourself a reputable dealer, luv."

"Actually, my younger brother, Theo, is an art dealer."

"Oh." Discouraged but not beaten, Miss Adler carried on. "Well, obviously in some dirty little backwater city, eh?"

"Paris. I send him my paintings, but he cannot sell them. It's mystifying that no one, not a single person has bought any of my work. It is only through Theo's generosity that I can continue to paint. He sends me money and supplies."

This revelation put a decisive end to Miss Adler's hopeful speculations, and it was clear to me that the time had come to bring this pointless exercise to an end. "Well, thank you so much for stopping by with your most interesting story, but I'm afraid this is a professional consulting agency. We charge all of our clients a fixed fee—"

"—except when we remit the fee altogether," Holmes chimed in.

"Which we're not doing anymore!" I chimed right back.

At this, Van Gogh became excited and somewhat agitated. "But I have brought you payment! I brought you a piece of my work."

Van Gogh retrieved the wrapped painting he had carried with him all the way from Arles and offered it to Holmes, who accepted it with a smile. "Well, that's very gracious of you, Mr. Van Gogh. Very thoughtful."

"Holmes..."

"Now, now, let's just have a look, shall we? The fellow's travelled all this way with half an ear, after all."

Holmes then proceeded to unwrap the painting, revealing the most peculiar piece of art I had ever seen in my life. It was composed almost entirely of blue and yellow splotches of paint in thick, wavering lines which suggested that some kind of drunken seabird had strolled across the canvas. I could pick out what I supposed was a small town on the edge of a body of water, along with two small figures in the foreground, which I gathered were intended to represent human beings of some kind.

Van Gogh caressed the frame as if it was his own small child. "I call it, 'Starry Night over the Rhône.' I painted it a few months ago while standing on the banks of the Rhône River...it is only a minute or two walk from my house in Arles."

"How much absinthe were you drinking?" I asked.

"I'm sorry?" Van Gogh seemed mystified by my question as I became aware of Miss Adler moving closer to the painting, almost in a trance. I could see that she was trying to master some kind of powerful emotion, but she couldn't disguise the tears that were welling up in her eyes. When she spoke, it was with no trace of her Mrs. Hudson character's Cockney accent. "You'll have to excuse Dr. Watson...he's a medical man. It's all facts and science to him. He doesn't have the soul of an artist, which you, Mr. Van Gogh, most definitely do."

Van Gogh looked at her in gratitude. "Why thank you..." He paused, his brow furrowing slightly. "What happened to your accent?"

"Oh..." Miss Adler wiped away the single tear that had threatened to run down her cheek. "...it's not really an accent as such. It's more of a sinus infection than anything. Now please…describe to us what we're looking at."

"Very well." Van Gogh closed his eyes, seeing it so clearly in his mind that he had no need to gaze upon the painting itself. "The sky is aquamarine. The water is royal blue, the ground is mauve, and the town is blue and purple. The gas is yellow and the reflections are russet gold descending down to green-bronze. On the aquamarine field of the sky the Great Bear is a sparkling green and pink, whose discreet paleness contrasts with the brutal gold of the gas. Two colourful figurines of lovers are in the foreground."

Despite the bizarre appearance of the painting, it was quite a beautiful little speech, almost an incantation, and I could see that even Holmes was affected. "And may we presume that you are one of the lovers depicted, Mr. Van Gogh?"

Van Gogh opened his eyes. "I can see that I have come to the right man. You must help me, Mr. Holmes."

Miss Adler took the painting from Holmes and spun away from us, drinking in every last detail of it. Even as Holmes watched her, he addressed Van Gogh. "I'm still unclear in what manner I may be of assistance."

"It has to do with my ear. Or rather, the missing part."

"Go on."

"The woman in the painting..."

"Is Rachel, of course."

"Of course," agreed Van Gogh. "Every night we would stroll along the banks of the Rhône, and I wanted to capture those moments for her...for us. Life is so uncertain, so temporary. And none of us can be certain what the morning will bring. But I fear that I may not have been completely truthful with you about Rachel and the nature of our relationship. You see, the fact of the matter is..."

Here Van Gogh paused, unable to go on, but it was then that Miss Adler turned around to face us. "She's a whore."

Holmes and I both jolted slightly at her directness, but Van Gogh took it in stride. "The French have a more pleasant expression...*une fille de joie*."

"And I'm sure that makes it much more pleasant for the women."

"You'll have to excuse Mrs. Hudson," I explained to Van Gogh. "She's a bit of a—"

"Sentient human being sickened at the exploitation of women for the pleasure of men? Is that what you were about to say?" The look in Miss Adler's eye told me very clearly that it would be best if I retreated from this particular field of discussion, and so I did what I often did in these situations, pretended to take notes. However, should the reader be curious, I should mention that Miss Adler did not disapprove at all of my occasional visits to see Mrs. Nesbitt, quite sensibly referring to her as a "professional businesswoman who conducts her own affairs," which was indubitably true.

"Please don't imagine that I am proud of my actions," continued Van Gogh. "Ya, I keep the company of whores, but what choice do I have? I am not an attractive man, a wealthy man, a famous man. I have a great fire in my soul, but no one ever comes to warm themselves at it...and the passersby see only a wisp of smoke in the distance."

Van Gogh fell silent, lost in some internal reverie, and I caught a glimpse of the despairing, tragic figure behind his piercing blue eyes. I saw Holmes glance at Miss Adler, whose lower lip had begun to quiver, deeply affected by the unfathomable depths of loneliness that Van Gogh had just described to us. And then, with a shuddering breath, Van Gogh went on.

"But Rachel, she is different...far different from anyone I have ever known. She will talk to me, spend time with me, and lay her hand gently on my arm to calm me and take my mind from darker thoughts. Most of all, she likes my paintings. God bless her, she likes my paintings. You see, I have spent my life looking for a different light, a brighter sky, and that is what I found in Rachel. In fact, since she arrived in Arles I have given her most of my work, because she is the one person who has seen past my ugliness...and I would even venture to say that she loved me..."

"Until the arrival of Paul Gauguin." Holmes' logic was as incisive as it was brutal. Van Gogh staggered slightly, reaching towards the divan for support, and Holmes and I rushed to help him.

"Are you all right?" Holmes asked.

"I am very tired. I have barely slept these past four days. It was no easy matter getting here, of that I can assure you, but I knew that I must see Sherlock Holmes to have any chance of a shred of happiness in my life."

The ringing of our bell broke the spell that Van Gogh had woven, and even Holmes seemed taken by surprise. "Who the devil can that be?"

I rushed to the window, looked down, and saw a woman dressed entirely in black below.

"It's another client, Holmes! A woman!"

"Well, we can't see her just now—"

"A very fashionable woman!" I hoped Holmes would pick up on my hint, but it was clear he had Van Gogh's difficulties on his mind.

"Watson, you surprise me. We don't discriminate between clients based on their fashion sense."

"What I mean is...she's exceedingly well-dressed." I emphasised these last three words by rubbing my fingers together in the universal sign for money.

"Oh," replied Holmes, light finally dawning, "that kind of fashionable."

Momentarily nonplussed, Holmes turned to Miss Adler for guidance, which she readily provided. "Mr. Van Gogh is in no state to continue his story. He needs to rest."

"Absolutely!" I agreed, thinking of the prospect of a paying client standing on our doorstep. "Thank you, Mrs. Hudson!"

Taking Van Gogh's travelling case, I guided him towards my bedroom where he could recover a little from his ordeal. He had no sooner stretched himself out on my bed than he was asleep, and I covered him with a blanket to help keep him comfortable. Looking at his sleeping form, I felt that I could almost see his features relaxing, and it occurred to me that it was not really all that long ago that his mother and father had looked down upon him as a baby or small child. Like any parent, they would have had no inkling what the future held for him, but I doubted that they could have ever imagined their son compulsively painting in the South of France and slicing his own ear off for the love of a woman.

By the time I returned to our sitting room, I could hear Miss Adler bringing our new visitor up the stairs, thankfully with no trace of a Cockney accent. A moment later she entered with a woman clearly in mourning, as she was clad head to toe entirely in black. Even her veil, gloves, and small purse were of the same dismal hue. With our day quite clearly underway, Miss Adler excused herself to change clothes, and as our visitor hesitated just inside our door, Holmes moved towards her, "Please, do come in."

Taking her by her left hand, he guided her to the centre of the room. "I am Sherlock Holmes and this is my colleague, Dr. Watson. You've already met our housekeeper, Mrs. Hudson. And you are?"

From beneath the veil came a soft yet strong voice with a French accent, "My name is Marie Chartier."

Chapter Four
The Mysterious Marie Chartier

Holmes and I shared a quick glance, a glance that conveyed our mutual and instant first impression—this was no ordinary client. It was there in her voice and her bearing, but that didn't mean that Holmes would stray from the protocol which closely dictated his words and actions upon the arrival of a new client. First and foremost, as most clients come to us because of events ranging from suspicions to disasters, it was essential to put the client at ease.

Holmes was a master at this—attentive and gracious— regardless if it were a Dutchman with half his ear missing or a Frenchwoman in mourning. No matter how rough the seas might be outside of our rooms, within 221B there was a safe haven for anyone seeking it.

"Well, Miss Chartier," began Holmes, "I don't know what manner of concern or trouble has brought you to our doorstep, but let me assure you that you are among friends here."

Miss Chartier started slightly, "How do you know I am not married?"

"I detect no wedding ring beneath your glove. Am I incorrect?"

As Miss Chartier shook her head, Holmes continued, "You appear to be in some degree of distress. Please, take a seat."

Guiding Miss Chartier to the divan, she sat down with her hands clasped and head bowed. As Holmes settled himself in the armchair, I pulled out my notebook and pencil.

"I see that you are in mourning, Miss Chartier," Holmes said. "Is there some connection between the death of a loved one and your visit here?"

"Yes."

"Then if you'll forgive my asking, who is it that has passed away?"

"My father."

"Ah. I'm very sorry to hear of your loss."

Instinctively, my heart went out to the poor woman. "Quite. A terrible thing losing a parent. Our deepest condolences."

"How was it that he came to pass on?" asked Holmes.

"He was murdered."

"Murdered? Are you certain?" To this, Miss Chartier only responded with a slight nod and Holmes continued, "Have you contacted the police?"

"No."

"Why not?"

With that, Miss Chartier swooned where she sat, collapsing against the back of the divan.

"Holmes, she's unwell!"

Miss Chartier raised a gloved hand, "If I might have a glass of sherry."

"Of course!"

There are few things that galvanise any gentleman quite so much as a lady in distress, and so I fairly leapt to the sideboard to fetch her a glass of sherry. Already intrigued by the unusual answers he was receiving, Holmes pressed on.

"I must confess myself slightly confused, Miss Chartier. You say your father was murdered, but the police are not involved?"

"No."

"Well, I will admit they do have their shortcomings, but Scotland Yard has several fine detectives. And if they find themselves struggling with a case, it's then that they come to me."

"Scotland Yard is of no use to me. My father was not murdered in this country."

At this I arrived with Miss Chartier's sherry, and she removed her hat and veil. It was, I must say, a quite stunning transformation, as if dark clouds had been swept away to reveal a shimmering rainbow beneath them. I don't think I have ever seen a woman so exquisitely, so effortlessly beautiful. Auburn hair framed her face in gentle ringlets and her green eyes, remarkably, seemed to have filaments of gold radiating from her pupils to the perimeter of her irises. The effect, I must say, was utterly bewitching, and as she sipped her sherry, she looked at me curiously.

"Is something the matter, Dr. Watson?"

"No! No, no, no, no. Just wondering...wondering if you're enjoying that sherry!"

"It is most pleasant, thank you."

Hearing a bedroom door close behind me, I observed Miss Adler slipping back into the room wearing a simple, yet very becoming outfit. Spotting Miss Chartier's hat and veil, Miss Adler dutifully played the role of housekeeper and picked them up, brushing the hat off and placing it on our hat rack. For some reason, Miss Adler's reappearance put Miss Chartier even more on edge, and she stood up abruptly.

"I should not have come. I am wasting your time. There is nothing you can do and I am intruding—"

"Not at all!" I fairly blurted out.

"Are you certain? If you could spare me a few moments of your time, I can pay whatever you ask." Miss Chartier reached into her purse and removed a thick roll of banknotes tied with a ribbon. "Perhaps one thousand pounds as a retainer? Would that do?" As I gaped in amazement, Miss Chartier set the money down and addressed Holmes. "But I know how much you value the strange and fantastic in your work. Perhaps this case would not be attractive to you."

"It's attractive!" I assured her. "Very, very attractive."

"Or perhaps you would not wish to travel to another country to investigate—"

"Nonsense! Holmes and I adore travelling! We love the wind at our backs and a bit of dust in our throats, don't we, Holmes?"

Before Holmes could answer, Miss Adler turned from the hat rack, still in the character of Mrs. Hudson, but without the dreadful Cockney accent. "Will you be wanting the chicken or the smoked salmon for lunch today, Mr. Holmes?"

The question took me by surprise, as Miss Adler did not number cooking among her interests, abilities, or accomplishments.

"We're actually in the middle of a case," I began. "This is Mademoiselle Marie Chartier. Miss Chartier, our housekeeper, Mrs. Hudson."

It was then that a most remarkable thing occurred, as I could almost feel the temperature in the room go up by several degrees. Almost instinctively, Miss Chartier and Miss Adler began to circle one another like tomcats in heat. Proficient in several languages, Miss Adler proceeded to address Miss Chartier in her native tongue.

"*Ça va?*"

"*Ça va.*" Miss Chartier was observing Miss Adler closely. "*Parlez-vous français?*"

"*Un petit peu.*"

Anxious to get back to the case, I endeavoured to catch Miss Adler up. "Miss Chartier has suffered a personal tragedy and has come to us for counsel and help."

"Her father was murdered abroad," added Holmes.

"Indeed?" Miss Adler didn't seem surprised in the least. "In Europe, I would wager."

"Well, we don't know where, exactly—" I began.

"No, Mrs. Hudson is correct," confirmed Miss Chartier.

"Ah, I see. The French accent, yes? So, it was France, then?"

"No," Miss Adler continued. "And not in one of the large countries. But not one of the very small countries either. Somewhere in between. Let's see...what's a nice-sized European country where they speak French? Switzerland, perhaps?"

Improbable as it might seem, this elicited a small smile from Miss Chartier.

"I see from your reaction, Miss Chartier," observed Holmes, "that Mrs. Hudson has scored a palpable hit."

"I'm just a good guesser," said Miss Adler.

"I can see that," agreed Miss Chartier.

"And I'll tell you something else, Miss Chartier. Knowing Mr. Holmes' interest in the singular and unexpected, I assure you that he will be most interested in your case."

Apparently this was news to Holmes, who looked up in surprise. "I will?"

"You will," continued Miss Adler. "Because it's not every day that you meet a woman whose father died in such spectacular fashion; specifically, plummeting to his death from the top of a waterfall...the Reichenbach Falls, to be precise..."

Now then, it is true that I have been accused, on more than one occasion, and by more than one commentator, of being a little slow on the uptake. Certainly, in comparison to Sherlock

Holmes or Miss Adler, I have trouble making the logical leaps which they accomplish with effortless grace as I trundle slowly behind in their wake. Still, for all that, I would venture that I am not slower than the average fellow, and I will say in my defence that it should be remembered that even when I am in the middle of a case or a life-threatening situation, I am always thinking about how I might best relate it as a story.

This is the way writers live our lives, simultaneously participating and observing, and it's true that I can get somewhat distracted from the matters at hand as I silently search for just the right word to convey what I am witnessing or experiencing. In this particular instance, I will confess that I did not exactly cover myself in glory upon hearing Miss Adler's revelation, as the first words out of my mouth were, "The Reichenbach Falls? Why, that's where Holmes threw Professor Moriarty to his death!" Reading that now, it does sound faintly ridiculous, but in the heat of the moment it was all I could think to say.

"Yes. That is exactly what he did." And as Miss Chartier pulled a single-shot derringer from her purse, it all came to me in a rush. "You're...good Lord! You're Professor Moriarty's daughter? Holmes, did we know Moriarty had a daughter?"

"We do now."

Miss Chartier turned her full attention to Miss Adler. "I am most impressed. What gave me away?"

"Your name, of course. Moriarty is merely the Anglicised form of the Gaelic name Ó Muircheartaigh, which means 'navigator' or 'sea worthy.' 'Muir' means the sea, much like the French 'mer,' and 'Cheartaigh' means correct or worthy. The French version of the name becomes obvious...Marie Chartier."

"Bravo!" Holmes was beaming with pride. "Outstanding, my dear! You've outdone yourself."

"Not really. I'm afraid that you and Dr. Watson allowed yourself to be distracted by a pretty face."

"What? No!" I protested. "Nonsense! Not at all!"

Miss Chartier pivoted towards me slowly, like a cannon seeking out a new target. "You do not think that I am beautiful?"

"I didn't say that! Women with guns are always quite striking. Wouldn't you say so, Holmes?"

"Quite. And unlike the pure and chaste Dr. Watson, I will confess that the aesthetically pleasing qualities of your appearance did momentarily cloud my deductive faculties. Fortunately, we have Mrs. Hudson on hand for such eventualities."

"Indeed," Miss Chartier turned her attention to Holmes. "I have long waited to meet you, Mr. Holmes. You were the last man to see my father alive."

"Yes..." I could see that Holmes was struggling for what he might say next. "...an exceedingly regrettable incident, Miss Chartier."

"Not for you."

"Your father...forgive me, but I'm not certain just how much you know about him."

"I know that he was an esteemed professor of mathematics. I know that he wrote an influential book titled 'The Dynamics of an Asteroid' and a treatise on the Binomial Theorem. Most importantly, of course, I know that he was my father and that he loved me and I loved him."

"Miss Chartier," I began, "everything you have said about your father is quite true. That he was a brilliant man is beyond question. However, I hasten to add that oftentimes our parents have entirely separate lives of which their children know nothing."

"What are you implying?"

"Simply that…well, as you might imagine, if your father came to the attention of Sherlock Holmes, then there was more to his character than a simple professor of mathematics."

"I do not know what you can mean. All I know is that my father was often in Switzerland on banking business, as that was where I was conceived and born. Sadly, my mother did not survive childbirth, but my father saw to it that I received the best education that money could buy. On this occasion, the last time that he came to Switzerland, he was attacked by Sherlock Holmes at the Reichenbach Falls and brutally murdered. Why should you do such a thing, Mr. Holmes?"

It was not often that I saw Holmes speechless, but this was one of those occasions. He had to offer up some explanation, or it would appear that he had capriciously killed Professor Moriarty in cold blood for no reason at all. On the other hand, he couldn't very well tell Miss Chartier the truth about her father and speak ill of the dead. I could feel myself literally holding my breath, having no idea how the situation could possibly resolve itself, until Miss Adler spoke and cut through the tension like Alexander the Great's sword slicing through the fabled Gordian Knot.

"The answer to your question is quite simple, Miss Chartier," she began. "Your father was a criminal. But to say he was a mere criminal doesn't do justice to the man. He was, perhaps, the greatest criminal the world has ever known, ruling London's underworld as if it were his own private army. He organised major crimes here and on the Continent, bribed the police and politicians, and enforced his rule through murder, beatings, and blackmail.

"The only man who realised the extent of his evil, and the only man capable of stopping him, was Sherlock Holmes. And so Mr. Holmes, at great personal risk to himself, took on the task of dismantling your father's criminal empire. Your father's response was precisely what one would expect from a trained mathematician—in this particular equation the only solution was for Sherlock Holmes to be killed.

"Not wishing to endanger anyone else, Mr. Holmes fled to the Continent, with Professor Moriarty and his thugs close behind. At length, your father lured Mr. Holmes to the precipice above the Reichenbach Falls, intending to hurl him into the abyss. However, he had made a fatal miscalculation. Thanks to Mr. Holmes' familiarity with the martial art of bartitsu, he was able to overcome your father and threw him to his death, at which point the world almost instantly became a better place."

"It's actually called 'baritsu,' Miss Adler," I found myself saying.

"No, it isn't," she returned with disconcerting confidence. "I suggest you look it up when we're done here."

She pointed to Miss Chartier, reminding me that we were in the presence of a grief-stricken daughter with a loaded gun in her hand. Given that, Miss Adler's blunt, but entirely truthful assessment of Professor Moriarty was breathtakingly bold, to say the least. I was already calculating what my first action would be should Miss Chartier decide to fire her gun, but instead, to my complete astonishment, she merely smiled.

"But then, I'm not telling you anything you don't already know," continued Miss Adler. "Isn't that right, Miss Chartier?"

"My father was a genius," returned Miss Chartier. "And the minds of geniuses cannot be expected to be confined within one small discipline or profession. In fact, I recall reading that within an eighteen-month period, Isaac Newton revealed his Laws of Motion, invented calculus, and built the first reflecting telescope as well. My father was no different, and turned his attention to any number of activities that stimulated his intellect and attracted his interest."

"Wait," I found myself saying, "you mean to say that you know your father was the Napoleon of Crime?"

"Of course she does," confirmed Miss Adler. "In fact, I suspect that her entire mourning outfit was purchased expressly for her visit here. Certainly her hat, which I just hung up, is brand new and not of Swiss manufacture, for the lining bears the label of Crooks & Hanley."

"Why, that's a shop just two blocks over!" I said.

"And the vast majority of mourning daughters," Miss Adler went on, "would be unlikely to venture to a foreign city and enter the rooms of the man who killed their father armed with a gun and bent on revenge. But then, Miss Chartier is no ordinary woman. She is very much her father's daughter, and the dark impulses that blighted his existence run deep in her as well."

"What a remarkable housekeeper you are," said Miss Chartier.

"You're too kind," replied Miss Adler.

"And what a pity that my gun holds only one bullet, but that is all I need."

It was then, to my utter disbelief and horror, that Miss Chartier raised her gun, pointed it at Holmes, and smiled, "My father sends his greetings from the grave. *Adieu*, Mr. Holmes."

Fortunately, this gave Holmes a moment to prepare himself, and he dove out of the way just as Miss Chartier fired, with the bullet missing Holmes and embedding itself in our wall.

"*Merde!*" Tossing her now empty gun away, Miss Chartier pulled a sword from the wall and whirled on Holmes. I moved towards her, but when her sword hissed past my ear, I hurriedly backpedalled. "Stop this! Think of what you're doing!"

"I know exactly what I am doing." She took a step towards Holmes, then paused. "My name is Marie Chartier. You killed my father. Prepare to die." Such an exceptional line tempted me to reach for my notebook, even as Holmes scrambled to put some furniture between himself and Miss Chartier.

"Miss Chartier, may I be so bold as to point out that I have no weapon. Surely you wouldn't strike down an unarmed opponent?"

"And why not?"

"Well, it's not very sporting," I offered.

Miss Chartier practically spat out her contempt. "Being 'sporting' is for men. When women want to kill, they kill."

"That's quite true." Miss Adler agreed. "Women are treacherous..."

"...and deceitful..." added Miss Chartier.

"...and as a wise man once said, 'Not to be trusted, not the best of them.'"

Throwing a pillow at the still advancing Miss Chartier, to his credit, Holmes recognised when he was being quoted. "That was me! I said that!"

"Then we understand one another perfectly," continued Miss Chartier.

"Perfectly," agreed Miss Adler. "So you'll understand this."

And with that, Miss Adler reached down, took hold of the rug Miss Chartier was standing on, and pulled it sharply, sending Miss Chartier tumbling onto the divan, thereby giving Holmes a precious few seconds to secure a sword of his own. In a heartbeat Miss Chartier was back on her feet, and as Miss Adler and I edged away from the imminent conflict, Holmes held his sword in his left hand, waving it rather weakly.

It would be difficult to describe the sick feeling in my stomach as Miss Chartier closed in on Holmes. It was me, after all, who had described him as an "expert swordsman" in "A Study in Scarlet." To be honest, I really had no basis for saying that. Holmes and I had only just met, and while London does offer up a wide variety of entertainments and experiences, actual swordfights or duels are few and far between.

So, while it may have been a somewhat presumptuous conjecture on my part, I was simply hoping to convey to the reader that beneath Holmes' gentlemanly veneer, that he was a bit of a swashbuckler at heart. Still, given his many other talents, I had no reason to believe that he wasn't highly skilled with a sword in his hand, but as I heard the sound of steel upon steel, it quickly became clear that Miss Chartier was the far superior fencer.

Her footwork and body position were impeccable, giving Holmes the smallest possible target as she practically danced about the room, the sword flashing in crisp, controlled movements. Where on earth a Swiss girl could have learned to swordfight was the first question that sprang to my mind, but given who her father was, I was beginning to realise that Miss Chartier most likely had any number of surprising skills and talents. As Holmes scrambled for cover against her ferocious onslaught, the only thing in his favour was that Miss Chartier couldn't stop laughing.

"You call yourself an expert swordsman?"

"No, I don't!"

"It says you are in 'A Study in Scarlet!'"

"That was someone else's clever idea!"

"Just a bit of literary licence," I tried to explain.

"Literary licence which is about to get me skewered!" By this point Holmes was literally running away from Miss Chartier. It was, in truth, a painful thing to witness, and it is a painful thing for me to write. Holmes is supposed to be the hero, and heroes aren't generally characterised by scampering around pieces of furniture feebly waving a sword to no good effect.

I would much prefer that this passage were filled with colourful prose comparing Holmes to d'Artagnan from Dumas' "The Three Musketeers" or perhaps Robin Hood or Blackbeard the pirate. As my exasperation finally came to a head, I heard myself shouting, "For God's sake, Holmes! Stop running away! She's only a woman!"

In retrospect, not my finest moment, especially considering the two quite exceptional women currently in the room. It did have the effect of stopping Miss Chartier in her tracks as both she and Miss Adler turned death stares upon me. If he'd had any sense at all, Holmes would have taken the opportunity to flee down the stairs and into the street, but even he was struck into stunned immobility by what had just passed my lips.

"Sorry," I heard myself mumbling. "Very sorry. Do carry on."

Once again, Miss Chartier advanced on Holmes, who, in fairness, may not have possessed any particular swordsmanship skills, but proved quite adept at interposing pieces of furniture between himself and the increasingly frustrated Miss Chartier. As they both paused to take a breath, inexplicably, I saw that Holmes had a smile on his face.

"Well, I must say, this has been most invigorating."

Miss Chartier's eyes narrowed in suspicion, "Why are you smiling?"

"Because I know something you don't know."

"Ah...very clever, Mr. Holmes. You are not left-handed."

"No, sadly, I am left-handed. However, I am not the fencer in the family."

And with that, Holmes tossed his sword to Miss Adler.

Chapter Five

A Duel to Remember

Without seeming to even look at the sword flying towards her, Miss Adler somehow managed to catch it by its hilt, eliciting a laugh from Miss Chartier. "Seriously? Your housekeeper?"

I was as surprised as Miss Chartier, because again, in the day-to-day hustle and bustle of living in London, there are relatively few opportunities to engage in swordplay. I had no idea that Miss Adler possessed any skill with a sword, and what followed was perhaps the most astonishing scene I have ever witnessed in my life. I will confess that it is with some relief that I can describe what followed in its full, uncensored form. First, with deliberate calm, Miss Adler removed her top, revealing a bustier and corset beneath. Seeing this, Miss Chartier did the same thing, then proceeded to remove her skirt as well, revealing a short black slip and black stockings.

It would be indecorous to go into more detail than that, but suffice to say, given the danger of the moment and the provocative attire of the combatants, it was a most riveting spectacle. Having just witnessed Miss Chartier's prowess with a sword, I must say that I feared for Miss Adler's life, but then in recalling her long stage experience in opera, it occurred to me that she had likely spent many hours not only watching fencing being rehearsed, but knowing her, being an active participant as well. With deadly calm, Miss Adler proceeded to lift up the hem of her skirt with her left hand, then tapped the tip of her sword upon the floor.

"*En garde*, bitch."

That certainly got my attention, and even Holmes looked a little taken aback at Miss Adler's bold language, but Miss Chartier proceeded to smile, not intimidated in the least, and flourished her sword in an elegant manner, then lunged suddenly at Miss Adler with no warning. Miss Adler easily parried the blow, and they proceeded to set upon one another like two characters straight out of a Dumas novel.

All that Holmes and I could do was try to keep out of the way to avoid being sliced to ribbons by a wayward thrust or riposte. Back and forth they went across the room, but despite her best and most energetic efforts, Miss Chartier could not pierce Miss Adler's defence. Finally, she paused for a moment to catch her breath, not merely frustrated, but well and truly baffled.

"Who are you?"

And with a beautiful air of utter sangfroid, Miss Adler replied, "I'm just the housekeeper."

With that, Miss Adler feinted towards Miss Chartier's body, then pushed Miss Chartier's blade to the side before reaching for the hilt and violently pulling the sword from Miss Chartier's hand. It had all happened in the blink of an eye, and now defenceless, Miss Chartier nodded towards Miss Adler.

"Most impressive. I do not suppose you will do the sporting thing and return my sword?"

"I don't think so. I just went to so much trouble to relieve you of it."

"Then what? You plan on calling the police?"

"No. I plan on killing you."

True to her word, Miss Adler took a step towards Miss Chartier, but before Holmes or I could move or even object,

Miss Chartier took hold of Van Gogh's painting and held it like a shield before her.

"You would not destroy a valuable work of art, would you?"

"Valuable?" I scoffed. "It's not worth a bloody thing!"

"But it has been offered as payment," said Holmes. "Surely we must respect that."

"I'll only put one hole in it," offered Miss Adler. "I promise."

Holmes wavered, "Well..."

"A very small hole."

"How small?"

"You won't even notice it. And we've got Van Gogh in the bedroom. He can patch it up, no problem."

"No," Holmes shook his head. "I may not know much about art, but my grandmother was the sister of Vernet, the French artist best known for his series of atmospheric paintings of the seaports of France. Art must be respected, regardless of its monetary value. Watson, guard the door, please."

I instantly moved to do Holmes' bidding, already calculating whether or not I could fashion this bizarre and unique encounter into another Sherlock Holmes adventure. Van Gogh and Miss Chartier were both clearly colourful and interesting characters, and the swordfight itself would be worthy of a page or two on its own, although regrettably, in the story it would have to be Holmes with the sword in his hand, not Miss Adler.

Still, even with the addition of Van Gogh's severed ear and Miss Chartier being the daughter of Professor Moriarty, the absence of any kind of mystery was clearly a problem. Loath as I am to admit it, as I took up my position at the door to prevent Miss Chartier's escape, I found myself rather hoping that she had one more card up her sleeve.

"And I'm afraid this concludes our pleasant *tête-à-tête*, Miss Chartier," continued Holmes. "If there is nothing more, I will contact my friend Inspector Lestrade to conduct you to Scotland Yard on a charge of attempted murder."

Miss Chartier's expression, I was encouraged to see, was one of amused contempt. "You need not bother. And on second thought, I do not think I will retain your services as a consulting detective." And with that, to my dismay, she picked up the roll of notes totalling one thousand pounds and waved it tauntingly at Holmes before thrusting it down the front of her bustier.

"I'm afraid you're misjudging your predicament, Miss Chartier."

"And I am afraid your deductive faculties have failed you, Mr. Holmes."

"How so? Mrs. Hudson has you covered with her sword and Dr. Watson is guarding the door. Your situation is impossible." Miss Chartier's only response was an easy smile, which seemed to disconcert Holmes. "Why are you smiling?"

"Because you are forgetting your own rule of deduction. 'When you have eliminated the impossible, whatever remains, however improbable, must be the truth.'"

"I'm afraid I don't understand," replied Holmes.

"Then allow me to demonstrate." Miss Chartier addressed each of us in turn. "Mr. Holmes, Dr. Watson, Mrs. Hudson, if indeed that is your name. This has been an intellectual treat, but I must now bid you a fond *adieu*." And then, to our astonishment, taking the Van Gogh painting with her, Miss Chartier proceeded to run towards the window, kicked it open, and then jumped through it, disappearing in an instant. Holmes, Miss Adler, and I all stood frozen for a moment in disbelief, but then hearing the loud whinny of a horse, we all ran towards the window through which Miss Chartier had just disappeared.

Through an incredible stroke of good fortune, she had landed in a hay cart that just happened to be right below our window, and as it sped down Baker Street, there was Miss Chartier in the back of it, covered in straw, but waving and blowing us kisses.

"Good Lord!" I exclaimed. "There's a bit of bloody luck! If that hay cart hadn't been right beneath our window, she'd be in pieces on the cobblestones!"

Judging from his expression, Holmes disagreed with my analysis, remarking, "Sometimes, my dear Watson, luck is the residue of design."

I'm afraid I only dimly registered his point, because the full meaning of what had just transpired was now growing more and more apparent to me, and Miss Chartier's bold escape was far more promising in terms of a potential story than her arrest. I was scribbling down details as fast as I could in my notebook, trying to remember every word that had been uttered and everything that had taken place.

Professor Moriarty's daughter! And not just any daughter. She was clearly just as brilliant and evil as the late Professor. Whatever dark impulses flowed within the Moriarty bloodline, they had blossomed into full flower in the person of Marie Chartier, who also just happened to be one of the most beautiful women I have ever seen in my life.

"Wonderful…wonderful…" In my enthusiasm at recalling her mad leap out of our window, I'm afraid I expressed my admiration out loud, and out of the corner of my eye I became aware of Miss Adler staring at me.

"Wonderful? She just tried to kill Holmes!"

"But she didn't! If she had, of course, that would have been a terrible tragedy. But she didn't and it's a wonderful story! Now then, how might she best be described? Perhaps...'When she lifted her dark veil, every lineament in her features spoke of a possessed creature bent on bloody revenge'...no, that's a bit much. Maybe...'Pulling the gun from her purse, she gazed on Holmes with coal black eyes devoid of any human emotion...' Yes, much better!"

"Her eyes aren't black," pointed out Miss Adler. "They're green."

"I'm well aware of that," I answered, "but if I decide to write this up as a story for 'The Strand Magazine,' which would their readers prefer, black eyes or green eyes?"

"Definitely black," agreed Miss Adler. "Literary licence wins the day again."

For his part, Holmes didn't appear to be particularly unsettled by what had just occurred, although I could see his brow furrowing as he lit his cherry-wood pipe. "So you think she came here to kill me?"

"I'm sorry?" I wasn't sure that I had heard Holmes correctly.

"Was that the purpose of her visit? My assassination?"

"Holmes, she fired a gun at you."

"But missed...from extremely close range."

Holmes strolled to the window and gazed down at the street, puffing at his pipe thoughtfully.

"What are you thinking, darling?" asked Miss Adler.

"I'm thinking motivation. What is her motivation to murder me?"

"You threw her father to his death off a waterfall?"

"Which a true psychopath wouldn't care about one way or the other. As our eloquent friend Watson just described her, she's 'devoid of any human emotion.'"

"But Holmes," I objected, "she came here with a loaded gun in her purse! Surely that suggests murderous intent."

"She's the daughter of Professor Moriarty, and if I may say so, not exactly the shy and retiring type. That means she most likely has more than her fair share of enemies here and on the Continent. Given that, I suspect she carries a gun with her on a permanent basis. And why the veil?"

"You're Sherlock Holmes!" I said. "She must have feared that you would recognise some family resemblance to the Professor in her features."

Holmes turned from the window and shook his head. "But she willingly revealed herself when you handed her the glass of sherry."

"Maybe she only wanted to be anonymous on her way here," offered Miss Adler. "That way there would be no other witnesses to confirm her visit."

"I wonder..." Holmes turned back to the window to look down on Baker Street. Miss Adler and I exchanged a glance.

"Wonder what, darling?"

"If I told you, you would fancy that I had become as deranged as our new houseguest..." Holmes turned from the window again, and what he said next was absolutely the last thing I expected him to utter. "What if she came here to steal our Van Gogh painting?"

I couldn't help but laugh. "Then she's bloody welcome to it! That atrocity? I wouldn't hang that up in a Home for the Blind."

"I'm not sure I follow," said Miss Adler.

"I'm not sure I do either," continued Holmes, "but there's something about the whole episode that doesn't ring true. Her arrival, her appearance, her actions...we're missing something. Of course, it's a capital mistake to theorise without data..."

"There is no data!" I exclaimed. "She took the painting, and the thousand pounds, I might add. All we have is her empty gun, a bullet hole in the wall, and a depleted bank account."

"No, Watson. There's more to this than meets the eye, and I suspect that our friend Mr. Van Gogh is involved in some way that is not quite clear to me. However, our knowledge of the modern art world is woefully inadequate for the task at hand."

"Then clearly, research is required," Miss Adler was already moving towards the door. "I know most of the major art dealers in London. Perhaps I'll pay them a visit."

Heeding Miss Adler's call to action, I headed for the door as well. "And as it happens, I am acquainted with the most cultured man in London, so perhaps I'll see if I can have a word with him."

"Excellent!" Miss Adler plucked my overcoat from the coat stand and held it out to me. "See if you can pick his brains a little regarding the world of painting here and on the Continent."

As Miss Adler and I donned our coats and hats, we turned back to Holmes.

"And what will be your contribution to our investigation?" Miss Adler asked Holmes.

"Babysitting our new Dutch friend, of course," I answered for him.

"Precisely," agreed Holmes. "Someone has to stay here in case he awakens. And it will give me time to mull over the facts of the case."

"Just have some fresh tea ready when we get back," said Miss Adler.

"And tidy the place up," I added.

To his credit, Holmes took all this in good stride, standing with his hands behind his back and observing us both with perfect equanimity. "Anything else? Either of you need some socks mended, washing done?"

"I think that about covers it," said Miss Adler as I offered her my arm.

"Shall we, Miss Adler?"

"We shall, Dr. Watson."

We proceeded down our seventeen steps towards the street, but at the eleventh step, we both froze, the same thought occurring to us. Turning, we went back upstairs and opened the door to see Holmes rooting around in the back of a drawer of the sideboard.

"And stay away from the cocaine!"

With a swift movement, Holmes closed the drawer and looked at us in shock. "I wasn't!"

Miss Adler and I shared a knowing glance.

"He was," I said.

"Definitely," she agreed. "He gets like this when he doesn't know what to do."

"I was just looking for my tobacco!" protested Holmes.

"Then perhaps you might find it where you always keep it..." began Miss Adler.

"...in the toe of the Persian slipper," I concluded.

Holmes waved us away as if we were so many gnats buzzing around his head. "Oh yes, of course! My mind's on the case..."

In five swift strides I was across the room, opened the drawer, and pulled from it a green morocco leather case, which I knew full well contained Holmes' drug paraphernalia. I slid it into my jacket pocket as I made my way back towards Miss Adler at the door.

"You're being ridiculous!" Holmes called after me. "Both of you! I do have some self-control, you know."

"Not much," replied Miss Adler, "which is why we love you."

"And get dressed, for God's sake," I added. "It's the middle of the day. Stop lounging around in your robe and pajamas."

"Get your pipe," said Miss Adler. "Sit down. And start thinking."

And with that, Miss Adler and I made our way back down the stairs and emerged onto Baker Street. We stood for a moment on the sidewalk, but before either of us could say anything, we both became aware of someone singing above us. Looking up, we could see that my bedroom window was opened just a crack to let in some fresh air, and it was from this that we could hear Van Gogh singing quietly to himself. For a man with such a guttural voice, he sang in a remarkably fine tenor, and I imagine it was some old Dutch folk tune that he had learned as a child:

"*Galathea, siet den dach comt aen*
Galathea, see the day begins
No, my love, await and linger
It is the starlight
No, my love, await and linger
It is the moon."

The singing faded away and as I looked at Miss Adler I could see that tears had once again welled up in her eyes.

"What is it?" I asked her. "What is it about this man that affects you so?"

She shook her head. "I'm not sure how I can even express it. I just feel that beyond his rough manners and appearance, he is a beautiful soul."

"Well, that's a good thing, yes? The world needs more of them."

"True," she returned. "But in this world, beautiful souls rarely survive long."

Just looking at Miss Adler gave me an unaccountable lump in my throat, and so I cleared it and changed the subject. "I must say, I had no idea you were so adept with a sword. Presumably you received some training as part of your opera or theatrical education."

"Presumably." Her smile was enigmatic. "But then, a true gentleman doesn't ask a lady her secrets."

I nodded in agreement, but of course the reality is that no writer is a true gentleman, or gentlewoman for that matter. For us, the world and everyone in it are merely material. From the powerful stirrings of first love to the abyss of grief at the death of a child, we writers are always measuring, recording, and never fully of any moment. It's not as if we cannot share in joy or sorrow, but there is always a portion of ourselves set apart.

On more than one occasion I have described my friend Sherlock Holmes as a "calculating-machine," often in a somewhat pejorative sense, I'm afraid. That comes from recognising in him the same qualities that I possess myself— keeping humanity at a distance in order to see it more clearly. I feel somewhat guilty about this tendency from time to time— perhaps a little inhuman—but those moments soon pass. And then I start writing.

In keeping with the notion of not asking Miss Adler her secrets, I made no enquiries as to precisely where she might be headed. She had never previously given any indication of close relationships with London's art dealers, but then Miss Adler was a woman of infinite discretion and many resources. I had no doubt that when we reconvened back at 221B, she would be a veritable fount of information about recent trends in modern art. As for myself, I was already curious about what my cultured friend might have to say on the very same topic. And so Miss Adler and I said our good-byes and headed down Baker Street in opposite directions.

Chapter Six

The Esteemed Member of the Albemarle Club

Despite the cold temperature and brisk wind out of the west, it was really quite a fine day. For the first time in a week I could see slivers of blue sky peeking through the grey clouds, which was a sight that always did my heart good. Looking around at my fellow Londoners as I walked, it was apparent that none of them were enjoying the afternoon very much. Their heads were down, eyes fixed on the pavement as they hustled along, some with their arms clasped about themselves, anxious only to escape the elements as soon as possible.

For myself, I took in a lungful of frigid air and set out at a brisk pace, glad to feel the rays of the sun on my face, weak as they might be. As my father had once remarked to me, there is no such thing as bad weather, only inappropriate clothing. Beyond that, extremes in weather make us appreciate those fine days when it seems as if nature itself has decided to gift us with the perfect amount of sun and breeze. Or perhaps that's an attitude more commonly shared by writers than the general public.

In fact, the previous year I had found myself trapped at a social function that was beyond tiresome and seemed destined to go on for eternity. Well-dressed people wandered aimlessly about a rather sterile ballroom engaging in the most banal small talk imaginable. I caught small snatches of conversation here and there...the Queen had apparently gone up to Balmoral for the weekend, Lord So-and-So's jacket appeared to be out of style, what to do about the damned Prussians, and so on.

Gradually, I became aware of a rather large storm building outside and made my way to look out one of the windows.

It was November, with the temperature not quite at freezing, and as the rain lashed against the windowpanes I could hear the soft crackle of sleet building in intensity. The wind was coming in powerful gusts, bending the trees in the garden at ridiculous angles, and just as I was engaged in a quiet reverie about the power of nature and the insignificance of humanity, I felt a presence at my elbow.

I turned to see a young man in his early twenties with brown hair, a thick moustache, and pale blue eyes. He held out his hand, "It's Dr. Watson, isn't it? I'm Herbert Wells. I'm going to be a writer too." We shook hands, and I smiled weakly, fearing the inevitable questions one gets from would-be writers, usually starting with "Where do you get your ideas?" and ending with the dreaded "Will you read my book?" However, to my shock, Wells simply nodded towards the window with a rakish grin on his face. "Fancy a bit of a blow?"

I was so taken aback that I laughed out loud and immediately reappraised the young fellow. The desire to experience extreme situations and avoid social functions of all kinds are very promising traits for any aspiring writer, and sure enough, within a few years Mr. Wells had published such works as "War of the Worlds" and "The Time Machine." We bundled up and headed out into the storm, and although the shrieking wind made conversation virtually impossible, we both enjoyed ourselves immensely.

My destination today was the Albemarle Club, perhaps a mile and a half from our rooms in Baker Street, and although I could have hailed a hansom cab at any time, I concluded that a brisk stroll would be just the thing to clear my constitution of a surfeit of Christmas goose and plum pudding. I had every expectation of finding the Irish poet and writer Oscar Wilde there, and he was the very man with whom I wished to speak. At that point in time, Wilde was nowhere near as famous as he would eventually become, but he was already somewhat notorious as a wit and provocateur, and the publishing of "The Happy Prince and Other Tales" earlier in the year had presaged a brilliant and eventually tragic career.

Upon entering the club, it was no trouble at all to locate Wilde, who was surrounded by the usual throng of people anxious to hear every witticism that sprang from his lips. He was dressed much as I remembered from our last meeting, wearing a pale silk shirt, a suit of maroon velvet, knee breeches, bows on his shoes, and a colourful ascot tie. Across the back of his chair I spied his cape, as well as a handsome pair of kidskin gloves on the table next to him. Also on the table was an absinthe fountain and a bottle of absinthe, presumably there to keep the famed Wildean wit well-fuelled for the delectation of the crowd hanging on his every word.

Wilde was, to put it mildly, an interesting fellow. He didn't have friends so much as he had acquaintances, and didn't have conversations so much as he delivered quips and soliloquies. Invariably, some bold wag would try to match Wilde's wit, but it was always a losing proposition, as unequal a battle as pitting a snowflake against an avalanche. Much like Holmes, Wilde possessed a ludicrously quick and agile mind, with a ready store of facts and information that spoke of a lifetime immersed in books of all kinds. We had met at a publisher's function earlier in the year and to my surprise we had gotten on quite well, most probably because he enjoyed talking and I enjoyed listening. He had expressed an interest in meeting Sherlock Holmes, but given the busy schedules of both men, the encounter had yet to take place.

However, given the events of the morning, today seemed to be especially propitious for just such an event, and so I stood on the periphery of Wilde's admiring circle for a few moments, then took a seat nearby. I was in no rush, for I knew that Miss Adler would need some time to work her magic with London's art dealers. I was thereupon treated to a steady stream of brilliant observations and *bon mots* on almost every topic under the sun.

Wilde flitted from one subject to another like a peripatetic butterfly, alighting here and there as he chose, but only for a moment before taking a sip of absinthe and moving on. Among many other subjects, he condemned the lamentable state of English literature, speculated on Robert Peary's failed attempt to cross Greenland two years earlier, and claimed that no civilised country would require its citizens to lick stamps for postage.

He then launched into a passionate defence of the American artist James McNeill Whistler's "art for art's sake" philosophy, making me feel even more certain that I had come to the right man. Eventually checking my watch, I observed with some surprise that no fewer than ninety minutes had flown by, and so I stood and moved to a position where I was in Wilde's line of sight. He spotted me almost immediately, and within moments he had dismissed his crowd of admirers under the excuse of a pressing assignation. He waved me towards a private side room, and within seconds he was shaking my hand vigourously, a searching expression in his eyes.

"Watson! Such an exquisite pleasure to see you! Surely you have better things to do than associate with the ne'er-do-wells of the Albemarle Club on a bleak Thursday afternoon."

"Not at all. I found your various disquisitions quite delightful and informative. However, the reason for my presence here is that we had a rather interesting morning in Baker Street involving a starving Dutch artist and a mysterious woman who is as beautiful as she is evil."

"Do tell!" enthused Wilde. "There are few human beings quite as compelling as a woman who has gazed into the abyss and who has then cheerfully jumped in."

"Well," I continued, "aside from music, Sherlock Holmes does not number the fine arts among his special areas of expertise, so I have been sent out into the streets of London in search of a man who does possess that knowledge."

Wilde smiled broadly, but only for a moment, as he was quite sensitive regarding the appearance of his large, misshapen teeth. "My dear Watson! You do flatter me, and yet, I must concur with your most excellent instinct. I am the very man you are seeking. I can offer you fascinating opinions on almost every aspect of today's art world, and if by chance we happen upon a topic with which I am unfamiliar, then I hereby give you my solemn word that I shall simply make something up."

"I don't doubt that for a moment," I replied, utterly charmed just as Wilde intended. "Then perhaps I can persuade you to accompany me to Baker Street for a brief consultation?"

"And will I meet the great Sherlock Holmes in person?"

"Indeed you shall."

"Then lead on Watson! I am yours to command!" Wilde called for his immense fur coat, a moment later I had hailed a cab in Albemarle Street, and we were soon on our way. Wilde seemed positively giddy at the prospect of meeting Holmes, but the rapid tapping of his forefinger on the frame of the window belied a certain nervousness as well.

"Do you think he'll like me?" Wilde said. "Mr. Holmes, I mean."

"Well, I—"

"I do like to be liked, and I will confess that I may be a bit too catholic in my tastes in that regard. I should be more discerning. I know that. As intoxicating as the worship of the mob may be, they can turn on a sixpence and positively revile you and call for your head on the end of a pike the very next day. It's a bit of a high-wire act, isn't it? Well, it is for me, at any rate. Every morning when I leave my rooms I fancy myself as an urban version of Charles Blondin, the French tightrope walker.

"He navigates a narrow rope stretched above the chasm beneath the Niagara Falls and I navigate the whirling and unpredictable waters of London's social scene. One moment you can be riding a wave of success and fame, and the next sucked down into a whirlpool of scandal and infamy, with your bloated and unrecognisable corpse pulled from the river weeks later. But then, I suppose this is the life that I have sought and deserve. Quite amusing how that works. Ah me....ah me, indeed."

And with that, to my utter astonishment, Wilde fell silent, apparently observing the unfolding kaleidoscope of London beyond his window, but I could tell that his gaze was inward, looking upon what scenes I couldn't imagine. Pulling up at Baker Street, I was pleased to see that our timing could not have been more perfect, for here coming towards us was the redoubtable Miss Adler. She had what appeared to be a wrapped painting under one arm and was shooing before her a young lad who was carrying two more wrapped frames. "Just here!" she cried and the boy came to a shuddering halt in front of 221B.

Wilde and I exited the cab, but before I could introduce him to Miss Adler, a well-dressed young gentleman across the street had waved to get Wilde's attention. With a wink, Wilde crossed towards him, saying, "Won't be a moment, Watson, old boy. Rest assured, I shall be straight up."

Turning towards Miss Adler, she brightened at the sight of me. "Dr. Watson! Help me get these paintings upstairs!" I duly relieved the young man of his burden, and as he held out his hand with the expectation of a tuppence or two, Miss Adler instead gifted him with a dazzling smile, pinched him on both cheeks, and kissed him on his forehead. "You are the most adorable thing I have ever seen! Thank you, my love!"

And with that she spun him around and propelled him back in the direction from whence he came. It was quite a sight to witness the poor boy staggering back up the street, his head turned to stare at Miss Adler, shock, hope, desire, and disappointment at not getting his tuppence all mingled in his expression.

"I believe the boy was expecting something more along monetary lines," I hazarded as I stood next to Miss Adler.

"Oh, he would have spent that before he even got back to the shop," she assured me. "And wouldn't you agree that some experiences are far better than a coin or two? Besides, aren't we economising?"

Now as ever there was little point in arguing with her, so we took our three wrapped paintings and ascended the stairs to 221B. Upon opening the door, we both suppressed the instant urge to call for the fire brigade as the room was utterly suffused with smoke. But then, this was Sherlock Holmes we were dealing with, and the stultifying atmosphere was no doubt the result of pondering a "three-pipe problem," as he sometimes put it.

Peering through the haze I could dimly make out the form of the gallant detective himself, stretched out on the divan fast asleep, with his deerstalker covering his eyes. He had managed to change out of his robe and pajamas, but that seemed to be the full extent of his exertions while Miss Adler and I had been bustling around London on the case.

Miss Adler set her wrapped painting down on the floor with more force than was absolutely necessary, and at that Holmes roused from his slumber and looked around in some mystification. "What's that? What's going on?"

Miss Adler stood before him with her hands on both hips. "You were sleeping!"

"No, I wasn't!" Holmes instinctively replied. "I was just resting my eyes."

"By sleeping!"

"Well, I may have dozed off just before you arrived."

Miss Adler wasn't having any of it, striding towards the window to open it and get some fresh air in. This managed to rouse Holmes to a greater state of consciousness. "Be careful! There could be assassins out there!"

A cold rush of air filled the room as Miss Adler ignored Holmes' warning and pushed the window open. "A bullet from an air-gun might kill me. The air in this room will definitely kill me."

Holmes turned to see me holding the two wrapped paintings, then cast a glance at Miss Adler.

"Paintings?"

"Research."

"Well, for Watson's sake, I hope you didn't buy those."

"Begged and borrowed."

"But not stolen?"

Miss Adler gave a shrug of her shoulders as she took a good look around the room.

"No tidying up, I see." And as Holmes opened his mouth to reply she immediately held up an admonishing finger. "And if you say anything about that being a brilliant deduction, you'll be a very sorry consulting detective."

"And the teapot," I added, "is stone cold."

All Miss Adler could do was shake her head. "And you call yourself an Englishman?"

"I was busy having productive thoughts!"

"You solved the case?"

"Not quite. A few details remain unclear. But I changed clothes!" Holmes twirled in an elegant pirouette, showing off his outfit.

"Very nice." Miss Adler looked Holmes up and down the way a butcher might appraise a side of beef. "I like that tie."

"Really? I picked it out because—"

"—you know it brings out that delicious shade of grey in your eyes."

"Does it?"

"It does."

Miss Adler moved closer to Holmes, running her hand along his cheek, and his eyes were riveted on hers. This, I'm sorry to say, was not an unusual occurrence in our rooms. I could be standing right there, as I was on this occasion, but it was as if I had completely blinked out of existence, at least as far as Holmes and Miss Adler were concerned. If ever an anthropologist wanted to write a treatise titled "Mating Habits of the British Detective," these scenes would have provided a veritable treasure trove of material.

With the Arctic blast still pouring through the window, I moved to close it, and glancing below, I could see Wilde still engaged in an animated conversation with his friend. Given that, I saw no harm in doing what I invariably do in situations such as these—I lingered to observe. Romantic attraction is, after all, part and parcel of the human experience, and I am a writer. Holmes moved his lips closer to Miss Adler's ear.

"Irene?"

"Mmm?"

"We are in the middle of a case, you know."

"That's exactly what I was thinking."

"About the case?"

"Indirectly. As you just said, a few details remain unclear..." Miss Adler was now tracing her finger around Holmes' lips. "...but that's only because you're not thinking clearly. And neither am I."

"And you're thinking..." By the second, I could see Holmes' cognitive abilities evaporating, and it was a fascinating thing to witness one of the finest minds in England struggling to string a coherent sentence together. "...thinking we might be able to help one another think more clearly about... about thinking?"

"One can hardly function at one's peak intellectual powers if one's most base animalistic desires are unfulfilled, can one?" Miss Adler accompanied her incisive logic by unbuttoning Holmes' shirt. "The mind will be distracted...with unbidden thoughts..."

"I'm actually having some of those thoughts, now that you mention it."

"Then what choice do we have?"

Out of the corner of my eye I spotted Wilde shaking hands with his acquaintance, and it was clear that their interview was coming to an end. Edging my way towards the door, I was descending the stairs a moment later, but I could still hear Holmes talking to Miss Adler, "So you're saying...what you're saying is...if I'm understanding you correctly...that it's our professional obligation to..."

And then I was back out in the brisk fresh air of Baker Street. I crossed over to where Wilde was standing, looking very pleased with himself.

"A friend?" I ventured.

"I should say so!" Wilde enthused. "Or an acquaintance soon to be a friend. He is an affable enough fellow, so why not?"

"Why not, indeed?" I concurred, not quite sure what he was talking about, but attempting to be agreeable nevertheless.

Wilde glanced up at our windows. "Is Mr. Holmes in? Is he receiving visitors?"

"Oh, I should say so. When I left him, he was engaged in a rather delicate chemical experiment with the assistance of our housekeeper, Mrs. Hudson."

"Then perhaps this is an inconvenient time."

"Nonsense! No time like the present, eh? This way. Now do tell me more about your writing routine. I would be most fascinated to compare notes with you."

Readers of a more judgemental disposition will surely condemn my inclination to have a bit of fun at Holmes' expense once in a while, but bear in mind that on one occasion, Holmes had the temerity to describe my sense of humour as "pawky." I like to think of myself as having a more well-rounded sense of humour than that, and this seemed like an excellent opportunity to prove it. Nevertheless, I am not of an unduly sadistic nature, and so as Wilde and I slowly ascended the steps towards 221B, I made a point of making a bit of noise and speaking more loudly than necessary as Wilde and I discussed our writing habits.

"So let me understand," I said to Wilde. "You spent the entire morning working on your volume of poems, and the only thing that you accomplished was removing a single comma?"

At his cheerful nod I burst into uproarious laughter and was gratified to hear a mad scramble of activity coming from our rooms.

"And what did you accomplish in the afternoon?" I asked Wilde.

"I put the comma back."

More uproarious laughter, and in this case I didn't have to fake it because that's actually quite a clever line, if I do say so myself.

When I opened the door, Wilde was so eager to get inside that he burst into our rooms ahead of me, like a butterfly emerging from its chrysalis. He spread his arms wide and looked about the place in absolute wonder, like a child on Christmas morning. Holmes and Miss Adler, I was pleased to see, were still in some degree of disarray, with Holmes straightening his jacket and Miss Adler tucking a wayward wisp of hair behind her ear.

Wilde, however, was oblivious to any traces of *in flagrante delicto* as he handed me his fur coat. In moving to hang it up, I was startled by the sound of a heavy object hitting the ground, and looked down to see the absinthe bottle he had somehow spirited out of the Albemarle Club. Putting it on the sideboard, I hung up his coat as Wilde toured the room in a state of ecstasy.

"Wonderful! Absolutely wonderful! It's just as I imagined! The deerstalker, the violin, the alchemy corner, the tobacco in the toe of the Persian slipper! And here, of course, the patriotic initials of our beloved sovereign marked on the wall in bullet holes! Victoria Regina!"

And with that, to my astonishment, Wilde launched into "God Save the Queen" with considerable enthusiasm.

> "God save our gracious Queen!
> Long live our noble Queen!
> God save the Queen!"

It felt a bit unpatriotic not to join in, so Holmes and I began singing as well, with Miss Adler conducting us with her feather duster.

> "Send her victorious,
> Happy and glorious,
> Long to reign over us,
> God save the Queen!"

Caught up in the spirit of the moment, I offered a hearty "Hip hip!" to which Holmes and Wilde responded with "Huzzah!"

"Hip hip!"

"Huzzah!"

"Hip hip!"

"Huzzah!"

Wilde gave a deep sigh of satisfaction. "Ah, I do love patriotism, even if it is a virtue of the vicious."

Chapter Seven

The Picture of Oscar Wilde

It must be said that if ever a man knew how to make an entrance, it was Oscar Wilde, and now that he had firmly established himself as the centre of attention in the room, introductions were in order. "Sherlock Holmes. Mrs. Hudson. May I present Mr. Oscar Wilde?"

Wilde bowed to Miss Adler and kissed the back of her hand, "A pleasure, madam." Turning his attention to Holmes, Wilde removed his gloves and approached him with an outstretched hand. "And the celebrated Mr. Holmes! And here I always suspected you were a fictional character!"

"I've had similar suspicions myself."

"Well, you know what I say. The only thing worse than being a fictional character, is not being a fictional character." Wilde removed his cape with a flourish and handed it to me, apparently having decided that I was the person in the room to whom things should be handed. "Now then, I am due to give a lecture very shortly, and so, Mr. Holmes, with your permission, I propose to spare you considerable time and intellectual effort.

"So let me just say, straightaway, that yes, I originally hail from Ireland, which you no doubt perceived despite my earnest and dogged attempts to eliminate all traces of an Irish accent. I cultivate an appearance of absolute idleness, yet work extremely hard, and I am married and the father of two young boys, but also a practising homosexual. Has anything escaped me?"

It's important to note here that Wilde typically spoke so rapidly and with such self-assurance, that his words often had the effect of a stream rushing over smooth stones with scarcely a ripple. Still, I found myself a little startled by something I had just heard him say, but wasn't quite sure that I had heard him say it.

"Hang on. You what?"

Wilde turned to me with a patient expression, as if he were used to this. "Work very hard."

"No," I persisted. "The other thing."

"I'm married?"

"Not that."

With the conversation veering in a potentially uncomfortable direction and with more pressing matters at hand, Miss Adler quite sensibly interposed herself.

"I think I might be able to clarify matters. Mr. Wilde is an Irish bugger." She then turned to Wilde. "I mean that in the best possible way."

Wilde smiled in acknowledgement. "I can't think of any other way."

I will admit that all this caught me a bit off guard and I found it necessary to reorient my impression of Wilde. In my mind, he had always been a witty, talented writer who enjoyed dressing up. Now, however, I found myself considering him in a new light and testing this old version of Wilde against the new version that had just been revealed to me.

The performance I had witnessed at the Albemarle Club had, of course, been for an audience composed entirely of men. Quite possibly, the young man who hailed him in the street may have had more than a word with an up-and-coming author in mind. Wilde's famous claim that he had kissed the poet Walt Whitman while on a tour of America became more than simply a flamboyant gesture.

In short, it all made perfect sense, and I inwardly chastised myself for not being more observant and open to the hidden possibilities that lie within any of us. I was aware that the death penalty for buggery had been abolished in 1861, but it was still considered to be a prosecutable offense, and so almost against my will I found myself saying, "Good Lord. That's illegal, you know."

Wilde took my comment in good stride. "Come now, do you seriously believe any civilised society would actually persecute someone based on their sexual orientation?"

At this, Wilde, Holmes, and Miss Adler burst into laughter, which took me a moment to decipher. It was, of course, blazingly obvious that practically every country around the world would quite happily persecute people based upon their sexual orientation, not to mention their race, religion, and so on. Persecuting people only slightly different from ourselves is, perversely and sadly enough, one of the great joys of an unsettling percentage of any population.

Ah, but then I picked up on the word that Wilde had quite purposely included in his question—civilised. In effect, he was declaring that England was not civilised, and I'm sorry to say that future events would prove him quite right. Still, in the moment, I could see that both Holmes and Miss Adler had warmed to Wilde and his disarming manner almost instantly.

"I like him," declared Miss Adler.

"As do I," concurred Holmes. "So allow me to meet your refreshing candour, Mr. Wilde, with a little of my own. This is Irene Adler, the American opera singer, and also my lover and confidante. Thanks to the unbounded discretion of Dr. Watson, she appears in the stories as our housekeeper, Mrs. Hudson, so as to not outrage the delicate sensibilities of the British reading public. As for Watson, he is as fine and patriotic an Englishman as you are ever likely to meet, but let's just say that that not all of his activities make it into his stories, especially those of a nocturnal nature."

Even as I was aware of a certain warmness in my cheeks and my collar becoming perhaps a shade tighter, Wilde clapped his hands in delight, "How wonderful! I feel much better now. We're all criminals with noble faces."

As was so often the case, Wilde's pithy remark contained within it an ocean of truth. Such was the genius of the man. In our typical day-to-day encounters with our fellow citizens, we usually assume that their lives are somehow simpler, purer, and more orderly than our own. But then, it only takes a moment or two of unguarded conversation, perhaps aided and abetted by a drink or two, and we find ourselves talking to someone with a troubled child, unfaithful spouse, or a worrisome malady that isn't getting better on its own.

Wilde's sexuality, our living arrangements with Miss Adler, and my friend Mrs. Nesbitt were scarcely topics for so-called decent conversation, but they nevertheless formed a part of our whole selves, and such secrets doubtless made up a portion of the lives of our friends and neighbors. Perhaps, I pondered, we might be a shade more charitable towards our fellow human beings if we were a little less concerned with keeping up appearances and measuring ourselves against unsustainable ideals.

Now that all of our respective masks had been summarily dropped, the atmosphere in the room was instantly warmer and more convivial. "May I get you a drink, Mr. Wilde?" asked Miss Adler. "What's your pleasure?"

"You're very kind. Sherry," replied Wilde, then he turned to me. "I say, Watson, were you contacted by a gentleman from 'Lippincott's Magazine' in America recently?"

"Why yes. How the devil do you know that?"

"Quite simple. I was contacted myself and he asked me to recommend any other writers that I knew. Of course, your name came immediately to mind. Apparently they're looking for material from sophisticated and proper English gentlemen such as ourselves."

Wilde accompanied his comment with a wink, and I must confess that it was incredibly flattering to know that he considered us to be in the same "club," as it were.

"Ah, now it all makes perfect sense," I said. "One of their editors, a man named Stoddart, I believe, contacted me out of the blue, said that he would be visiting England soon, and requested a meeting with me. I can't thank you enough for putting my name forward."

Miss Adler arrived with Wilde's sherry and after taking it, he held it out before him, gauging its colour with a connoisseur's eye.

"Not at all. You may not be the darling of the literati, damn their hides, but you tell a good, crisp, clean tale, Watson, with an excellent eye for detail and sense of place. I admire that. It's by no means as easy as it looks."

"Thank you!" I replied, with a reproachful look at Holmes, who upon occasion has been less than complimentary towards my literary efforts. "That's incredibly kind of you to say. So, will you be meeting with this Stoddart fellow as well?"

"Of course! One must always meet with American publishers. In fact, I have a proposition for you. What do you say to both of us conspiring to make his acquaintance simultaneously? We will overwhelm him with our British charm and civility, after which he will commission stories and bestow upon us large cheques."

"That sounds wonderful!" I enthused.

"Excellent!" Wilde pulled out a notebook and made a brief notation. "Then I propose dinner at The Langham Hotel. They have excellent claret and offer a fine rump of Cornish lamb. What do you say?"

"Why yes! Yes, of course! Thank you!"

Wilde waved my thanks away. "It's purely self-serving, I assure you. Should the American prove to be dreary, I will have you there to regale me with tales of Sherlock Holmes!"

Despite Wilde's flippant response, I greatly appreciated his kindness and thoughtfulness. He was an odd fellow, no doubt, but beneath the poses and gaudy attire lay an eminently decent human being.

"So, do you have anything in mind?" Wilde enquired.

"Anything in mind for what?"

"A story! Mr. Stoddart will be on a hunting expedition for stories. In fact, as he expressed himself to me, while a short story would be fine, ideally he's looking for something closer to novel length. Do you, perhaps, have a longer Sherlock Holmes tale that would fit the bill?"

"I'm not entirely sure that I do at the moment," I replied, fixing Holmes with what I hoped was a meaningful look. "I may have to browse through our old cases to find one that I can embellish a little. But one always hopes for new material, doesn't one? How about you, Wilde? Do you have a story idea in mind?"

"Oh yes! Yes indeed," Wilde pointed to his temple. "It's all up here. I'll just jot it down when I find a few hours of spare time."

"What's your story about?"

Wilde took a thoughtful sip of his sherry. "Just a silly little fable I have in mind. A mere fancy with which to amuse myself. It's about a brutally handsome young man who never grows old. However, he has a portrait of himself hidden in a locked room, and the portrait ages while he himself remains perfect and in the full bloom of youth as the years pass."

"Interesting," I replied, "but what's the point?"

"There is none," Wilde seemed absolutely delighted with himself. "Art needn't have a point. It need merely be beautiful and pleasing to the senses."

As if to punctuate his declaration, Wilde drained his sherry glass. Anticipating this, Miss Adler was right there to pluck it from his fingers. As she headed back to the sideboard to refill his glass, she gazed back at Wilde. "On the other hand, it could be seen as a story that serves as an indictment of our culture's worship of superficial appearances. And yet, Mr. Wilde's extremely stylish dress suggests that he is a dandy of the first order, therefore the story serves as both a warning and a catharsis for the tensions in his own life."

I had never imagined that I would ever see Wilde actually taken aback, as his intelligence and wit were more than enough to sustain him in even the roughest social seas. Still, it was clear that Miss Adler's remark had pierced his defences. I could see a dozen or so dazzling responses flitting behind his light blue eyes, but it couldn't disguise the fact that he was staring at Miss Adler in admiration bordering on adoration as she brought back his sherry glass.

"Did I mention that technically, I'm bisexual?"

I wasn't entirely clear if Wilde was joking or not, but this bold salvo roused Holmes from his well-practised attitude of studied indifference, "Excuse me? Did I mention that she's taken?"

"That would be my decision, I believe?" Miss Adler's tone was firm, but kind, and had the effect of making Holmes squirm uncomfortably for a moment before she let him off the hook. "I'm taken, Mr. Wilde. And in my experience, it's best to have only one brilliant and unstable lover at a time."

"Pity. I don't suppose there's a waiting list?"

"There is now."

While I enjoy a bit of flirtatious badinage as much as the next writer, here I will confess that I was feeling a little uncomfortable and out of my depth, and it was with some degree of relief that I remembered the paintings that Miss Adler had just acquired.

"I've got a wonderful idea!" I began, with more enthusiasm than was actually necessary. "It would appear that the resourceful Miss Adler has managed to acquire several examples of modern art. Perhaps we should take a look at them and try to understand what connection, if any, there might be between Marie Chartier and Vincent..." I hesitated, not wishing to humiliate myself in front of Wilde with my pronunciation of the Dutchman's last name, and Miss Adler mercifully came to my rescue.

"...Van Gogh."

Wilde immediately perked up at the name. "Van Gogh, you say?"

"Yes," said Holmes. "Do you know him?"

"I know of him. We have, apparently, mutual friends...to the extent that such a man has friends, of course."

"Do tell."

Feeling that we were actually getting somewhere, I brought out my notebook just as I caught sight of Van Gogh emerging from my bedroom. Unfortunately, I was the only person who could see Van Gogh entering the room, and so Wilde proceeded to describe him with a bit more brutal candour than was absolutely necessary.

"Well, most people, when they speak of Van Gogh, describe him as a madman, but that wouldn't be entirely accurate," began Wilde. "Van Gogh is not mad. However, his complete and utter mental disintegration does seem inevitable..." I knew Wilde was just getting warmed up and so I endeavoured to alert him to the presence of Van Gogh with a small wave, but was not immediately successful. "He wants to paint, but nobody wants his paintings—wants to love, but no one wants his love. Failed minister, failed art dealer, failed artist, dirty, moody, prone to fits, physically repulsive...yes, Watson?"

"Oscar Wilde, may I introduce you to Vincent..."

Van Gogh advanced towards Wilde, his eyes ablaze in fury. "Van Gogh!!! My name is—"

Van Gogh stopped abruptly, and for a bad moment I thought he was having some kind of seizure. Instead, he pointed to the sideboard, his entire demeanour softening in an instant. "Is that absinthe?"

Somehow, out of all of the bottles and other items crowded onto our shelves and furniture, the absinthe Wilde had brought with him was the only thing Van Gogh saw, summoning his full attention like a green beacon. With more than a little relief at seeing Van Gogh's rage deflected, Wilde moved towards the bottle and picked it up.

"Why yes! I was partaking of a glass or two at the Albemarle Club, and I must have absentmindedly brought the bottle with me. How silly."

Van Gogh was practically salivating, "If you don't mind, I would enjoy a glass."

"As would I!" Wilde turned to look at Holmes and Miss Adler. "You wouldn't happen to have an absinthe fountain, would you? Slotted spoons, cubes of sugar, that sort of thing?"

"I'm afraid not," answered Holmes.

Wilde wasn't deterred in the least. "Then we shall just have to rough it. Glasses?"

"I'll get some," said Miss Adler, heading to the sideboard.

Van Gogh's attention, meanwhile, had been drawn to the three wrapped paintings brought in by Miss Adler. "Are those paintings?"

"Indeed they are," replied Holmes.

"May I see them?"

"Drinks first!" Miss Adler arrived with a tray bearing glasses, and once again, Wilde's eyes shone in admiration. "My God, I love this woman! Anyone else fancy a wee nip, as the Scots folk might say?"

Holmes demurred with a slight shake of his head, as did Miss Adler, but as a writer I felt an almost professional obligation to try a glass. I was, of course, aware of absinthe's romantic and somewhat sinister reputation, but it was much more popular on the Continent than in England. Distilled from wormwood, of all things, it was the drink of choice for Bohemian artists in Paris, and it was particularly favoured by poets such as Baudelaire, Verlaine, and Rimbaud.

I had never sought it out, and always assumed that it was more useful to men moved by their poetic visions than a prose writer such as myself, who needs to avoid undue flights of fancy and compose a narrative that the reader can actually understand. After all, a Sherlock Holmes story written under the disorienting effects of absinthe was not likely to please the very proper and middle-class readers of "The Strand Magazine." Still, many writers and artists swore by its stimulating effects, and it was popularly known as The Green Muse, so this seemed to be the ideal opportunity to expand my horizons.

"I wouldn't mind a taste," I heard myself saying. "I've never had absinthe before. What's it like?"

Wilde proceeded to pour three glasses, passing the first to me, the second to Van Gogh, and keeping the third for himself, all while reciting the following, which I have to believe he had composed and rehearsed for occasions such as this: "After the first glass you see things as you wish they were. After the second you see them as they are not. With the third glass, tragically, you see things as they really are, and that is the most horrible thing in the world. Cheers!"

Wilde, Van Gogh, and I raised our glasses to toast one another, then proceeded to empty them in a single motion. In retrospect, I can say that sampling absinthe for the first time in the presence of two vastly experienced absinthe drinkers and endeavouring to emulate the easy way in which they downed their glasses was not the best decision I have ever made. The taste was of anise distilled down to its purest essence, and it was easily the most unpleasant eating or drinking experience of my life, and I say that as a man who consumed more than his fair share of army rations and the occasional roasted rodent while on duty in Afghanistan.

Absinthe, I quickly discovered, wasn't so much a beverage as it was a punishment for the sins of this lifetime and several previous lifetimes as well. Above feeling certain that every fibre of my being had been permeated by poison, it was everything I could do not to immediately hurl up everything I had consumed in the previous twenty-four hours. I was instantly nauseous, my throat spasming, eyes watering, and as I clutched for a nearby piece of furniture to steady myself, I saw Wilde proffering the bottle towards Van Gogh with a smile.

"Again?"

"Of course!"

At which Wilde refilled both glasses and they toasted one other, now apparently best friends for life. I wanted nothing more than to find a bathroom and then lie down for a bit, but at that moment Holmes clapped his hands together in apparent delight at our circumstances. "Well, this is ideal! We have both Mr. Van Gogh and Mr. Wilde to offer us their opinions on modern art. Irene, would you be so kind as to unveil the first painting please?"

Having survived a Jezail bullet in Afghanistan, I summoned my reserves to pull my notebook and pencil from my jacket to take notes. I did this with the full knowledge that my notes might not be as thorough and legible as I might wish, but if Van Gogh and Wilde were going to be critiquing these works of art, I didn't want to have to rely on my memory to accurately reflect their opinions. As Miss Adler removed the wrapping paper from one of the paintings, I glanced at Van Gogh and Wilde, who resembled nothing less than two hounds right before the start of a hunt, straining at invisible leashes and absolutely frantic to be let loose.

The first painting revealed proved to be an extraordinarily odd and off-putting scene that appeared to be set in a pub or café of some kind. Garish and ugly, the dominant tones were brown and green, and oddly enough, most of the people in the scene had their backs to the painter, which strongly suggested to me that they didn't particularly want their portraits done, at least by this painter. The men had hats and the women were barely more than outlines that had been sketched out, but apparently never finished, most likely because the artist realised that the whole canvas was a mess and simply gave up.

Most disturbing of all was a large woman at the right side of the frame whose flaming red lips and blonde hair were accompanied by a face that was of a blue-green hue. It was nothing short of ghastly, like gazing upon demons inhabiting a poorly lit circle of Dante's Hell, and if I should have ever had the misfortune to find myself in such an establishment, I would most certainly have turned on my heel to exit at speed. Wilde, on the other hand, positively lit up at the sight of the painting.

"Ah yes! My good friend Henri de Toulouse-Lautrec! I believe he calls this piece, 'At the Moulin Rouge.'"

Van Gogh took umbrage at Wilde's comment, his eyes squinting in disapproval as he began shouting. "Your friend? Don't be absurd! Lautrec is a friend of mine! I met him in Paris!"

"As did I! As have many people!" returned Wilde. "You will be fascinated to know, Mr. Van Gogh, that the city of Paris is not your exclusive province."

"Gentlemen, gentlemen," soothed Miss Adler. "This is not a competition. What can you tell us about this artist?"

"Lautrec is of noble blood—" began Van Gogh.

"—yet lives in the brothels of Montmarte," interrupted Wilde.

"He wears spectacles—"

"—and a bowler hat."

"He is quite short—"

"—with a normal torso, yet childlike legs."

"Ah! Ya, it is true! He has very short legs. But he has another physical feature known only to his most intimate friends, a feature which has given him a very special nickname. And that nickname is...?"

Clearly, Van Gogh felt that he had caught Wilde out as to who was the better friend of this Lautrec fellow, but Wilde merely smiled, letting the moment hang as he refilled both of their glasses, before calmly announcing, "Tripod."

Van Gogh's eyes went wide. "My God, you know Lautrec! To Tripod!"

At that, they both toasted one another and downed another glass of absinthe. Mercifully, I was not included in the toast, which gave me a moment to write down "Tripod" in my notebook, but by this point I had sufficiently recovered my wits to realise I had no idea what that was supposed to mean, aside from the possibility that this Lautrec fellow had taken up photography and invested in a tripod, as the painting business was clearly not working out.

I raised my finger, about to ask for clarification, when I caught sight of Holmes shaking his head, then noticed that Miss Adler had a peculiar smile on her face for some reason, as she set down the painting by Lautrec, then swiftly uncovered the second painting.

This one I recognised instantly. It was clearly the Eiffel Tower, but unfortunately painted by some poor soul who was losing his vision, if not already quite blind and painting the magnificent structure from memory. Was that a bridge in the foreground and perhaps a tree of some kind on the left hand side of the painting? And why the Eiffel Tower was largely an orange hue was anyone's guess, although presumably the poor artist had no idea what colours were where on his palette and just hoped for the best. Van Gogh was similarly unimpressed, and the painting's effect on him was as if someone had just struck him a violent blow. He shrunk back, shielding his eyes, "No, I cannot look at it!"

"Who is it by?" asked Holmes.

"A gentleman by the name of Georges Seurat," responded Wilde, "who favours a technique known as pointillism."

Van Gogh turned on Wilde in genuine anger. "It is not a technique! It is garbage! Dab, dab, dab, dab, dab. A thousand tiny little dots. What is that? Is that your soul? Can you paint your soul with tiny dots? No! For me, I dream of painting and then I paint my dream. Get that nightmare out of my sight!"

I can't say that I shared Van Gogh's physical revulsion to the painting, although it's certainly not something that I would ever hang in my room, or in any room for that matter. It was, how shall I put it, too fuzzy, and looking at it made me feel as if I needed spectacles. Still, it was apparent why Van Gogh had failed as an art dealer, where it's your job to coo and enthuse over whatever mess of oil on canvas you're supposed to pretend is art.

Miss Adler made her way to the third painting. "Well, Mr. Van Gogh, perhaps you'll have a higher opinion of this last painting." With that, she proceeded to remove the paper from yet another utterly bizarre canvas. It consisted of a quite disreputable-looking fellow with a beard and moustache standing in front of bright yellow wallpaper emblazoned with what appeared to be parrots riding balls of cotton. There was a green cartoonish silhouette of a bearded man in the upper right-hand corner, and I knew enough French to be able to decipher the writing below it, which read, "The Miserable Émile Bernard."

It was impossible to discern which of the gentlemen in the portrait was Monsieur Bernard, but neither one appeared unduly miserable, at least to my untutored eye. Perhaps sitting for the artist had made them miserable? That was certainly understandable if they happened to catch sight of the manner in which they were being depicted on the canvas.

Wilde nodded sagely as he considered the painting from various angles. "Ah yes, the notorious Paul Gauguin."

"Well done, Mr. Wilde," remarked Miss Adler. "You know the man?"

"Only slightly. Gauguin is a self-professed savage with a monumental ego. Used to be a stockbroker, adept with a sword, but now he's as poor as dirt. He recently abandoned his wife and family in Copenhagen to try to make a name for himself as a painter in Paris, then enjoyed some success at an artist's colony in Brittany, with the female students if nothing else. I understand he also had a number of successful dalliances with the native women in Panama and Martinique last year and is trying to reinvent himself as a Symbolist."

Up until now, Van Gogh had been silent regarding this third painting, but now he approached Miss Adler with his arms wide to take it from her. He held it at arm's length, taking in every inch of it, and I feared an explosion of bad temper that would send the painting hurtling out of our window or being dashed to pieces on the floor. Instead, when Van Gogh spoke, his voice was barely above a whisper. "Paul…he is a genius. This…this is what art should be. His perspective, his use of colour…do you see how passionate blood suffuses his face like an animal in heat?" Van Gogh turned towards us, apparently mystified that we weren't all turning cartwheels of giddy delight. "Can't you see? Are you all blind?"

Perhaps it was the effect of the absinthe, or perhaps it was my growing outrage at being told that any of these works represented "art," but by this point I had had enough.

"See what, exactly? That's not…what I mean to say is…look here…" Being nearest to the Gauguin, I pointed to it first. "The world doesn't look like this! Or the Tripod one! Or the blind fellow who dabs away as best he can! You call these paintings? They're nothing more than the scrawlings of demented, drunken children!"

I saw Van Gogh's eyes flash in anger as he turned on me. "Gauguin is a genius! Don't you dare speak of him that way!"

I raised myself to my full height, determined to make a stand for decent art. Besides which, I liked my odds of defending myself against an underfed Dutchman.

"He paints like a drunken child!"

"Genius!"

"Child! He's a drunken child!"

"A drunken genius!"

By this point Van Gogh and I were literally chest to chest, which is why I didn't notice the sword in Miss Adler's hand until I felt it brush against my chin.

"Would both of you like to keep your noses?" asked Miss Adler. As the sharp, cold blade hovered between us, Van Gogh and I had the good sense to nod our acquiescence. "Then I want you to stop all this nonsense. We're in the middle of a case."

Van Gogh and I stepped away from one another, but I kept one eye on him as Miss Adler put the sword back amongst the fireplace tools. In the meantime, Holmes had steepled his fingers together in his traditional thinking pose and addressed Wilde.

"Your opinion, Mr. Wilde? My colleague may have put it somewhat forcefully, but he does have a point. For centuries, paintings have served to record and replicate reality, whether it be a portrait or a landscape. Say about these paintings what you wish, but they do not attempt to accurately represent reality in any conventional sense of the term. Rather, they give, shall we say, an impression of reality."

"Quite so," replied Wilde. "Hence the name by which these artists are known—the Impressionists. That was the term bestowed upon the French artist Claude Monet by a critic some fourteen years ago. It was not meant as a compliment, yet the movement has grown and evolved since then, with some of the better known Impressionists being Pierre-Auguste Renoir, Edgar Degas, and Mary Cassat.

"Collectively, they established a new genre of art that thrills some and completely alienates others. However, for the sake of accuracy, I should point out that all of the gentlemen whose paintings we have before us, including Mr. Van Gogh, have moved beyond Impressionism and are more properly termed Post-Impressionists."

"And are all of these Post-Impressionists as poor and unrecognised as Mr. Van Gogh?" asked Miss Adler.

"By and large, yes," nodded Wilde. "For whatever reason, their work has not caught the popular fancy. But then, to be popular, one must be a mediocrity." And as I scrambled to jot down that particular witticism verbatim, I could see that Wilde was checking his pocket watch.

"And with that, I'm sorry to say that I have obligations elsewhere. I hope that I have been of some assistance."

"Indeed you have," responded Holmes. "We're very much obliged."

Wilde donned his cape and headed for the door. On his way there, he picked up his bottle of absinthe, but then turned and handed it to Van Gogh.

"To fuel your beautiful dreams, my friend."

As I helped Wilde on with his fur coat, Miss Adler regarded him thoughtfully. "One last question, Mr. Wilde. These Post-Impressionists, do you think their fortunes will ever change?"

With no ready quip or witticism at hand, I could see that Wilde was seriously considering Miss Adler's question. Finally, he spoke, "I wouldn't presume to predict the currents of public taste, madam. However, I will say this—that when I gaze upon these paintings, it only reinforces my belief that while we are all in the gutter, some of us are looking at the stars."

And with that, Wilde inclined his head in a slight bow and was gone.

Chapter Eight
A Whiff of Conspiracy

I will admit that as I got out my notebook once again to jot down Wilde's parting words, it was with a certain amount of reluctance, if not bitterness on my part. I would never make any claim to being in the same company as Shakespeare or Milton as a writer, but all things considered, I feel that I hold my own reasonably well. My descriptive powers are fairly decent, if not better than decent, and I like to feel that my tales have a good sense of pacing about them, so that the reader is both engaged and entertained. However, Wilde's ability to somehow manufacture brilliant lines out of thin air at a moment's notice was a bit maddening, if for no other reason than I am not that clever.

And the moment that thought crossed my mind, I was struck by the obvious—Wilde wasn't that clever either. He couldn't be, at least insofar as his instantaneous witticisms were concerned. My first inkling of this had been his set piece regarding the absinthe, but now I was starting to wonder just how many of these set pieces he had. I hasten to add that I am not in any way trying to dismiss his genius, but those brilliant off-the-cuff quips were surely the product of long nights spent composing those very same quips. They had to be. After all, how many different social situations does one find oneself in? How many topics of conversation are there? Besides which, people are most likely to remember the first thing you say when you arrive and the last thing you say as you leave.

There was, I began to realise, a distinct pattern, and I might even say an almost mathematical quality to the equation of being considered dazzlingly witty. Of course, now was not the time to fully consider the implications of this epiphany, as we were in the middle of a case, but I resolved to begin composing witticisms for every occasion at the next available opportunity, and committing them to heart. With any luck, my name would be mentioned in the same breath as Wilde's within a year or two at most. As I finished copying Wilde's parting observation into my notebook, Van Gogh took a swig of absinthe straight from the bottle and headed back towards my bedroom.

"Mr. Van Gogh! Where are you going?" asked Holmes.

Van Gogh turned. "Paul's work is an inspiration! God has hurled me upon this vast stage of human life, and I have yielded everything I felt beat in my heart and boil in my brain. I must paint!"

As he took another swallow of absinthe, I winced on his behalf and felt obliged to interject, "But Vinny, I say, perhaps leave the absinthe behind, don't you think? Everything in moderation, you know."

"Perhaps for you, Dr. Watson," he regarded the bottle as one would a beloved firstborn child. "For me, if the storm within gets too loud, I take a glass too much."

And with that, Van Gogh entered my room, slamming the door behind him. Now that parting line, I will confess, I found a bit disconcerting. It was good. Very good indeed. Had he said it before or heard someone else say it? Was I the only one apparently incapable of tossing off a quotable quip every time I exited a room? Feeling a bit of trepidation at pursuing that line of enquiry at the moment, it was with a certain sense of relief that I remembered our case, if in fact we even had one. There was no point in pretending that I knew better, so I simply turned to Holmes and Miss Adler and asked, "Which leaves us where, exactly?"

Holmes took Miss Adler's hands in his. "Shall we cogitate, my dear?"

"I would love to!" Miss Adler replied.

And again, in the spirit of full candour, I will confess that I made a bit of a fool of myself at this point, for I had misheard the word "cogitate."

"Not in here, you're not! For God's sake! A little decency, please. Just because we had Wilde here doesn't mean we don't have to conduct ourselves like civilised human beings! You're taking the entire Bohemian business too far!"

Holmes turned to me in surprise. "Watson, we're simply going to think about the case out loud."

"Oh! I thought you said...so you're not going to..."

"Unless you would like us to," remarked Miss Adler with a smile. "Do you number voyeurism among your vices, Doctor?"

"He is a writer," added Holmes. "That's practically their job description."

Being at a bit of a low ebb, I'm afraid that my reply was on the snippy side. "May I tell you something? Both of you? It's a jolly good thing the British public has no idea what goes on behind these four walls. We'd all be tarred and feathered and run out of the country, the lot of us! But my original question still stands. All of this leaves us where?"

"At a tipping point in the history of art," replied Holmes.

"What? How so? You're not suggesting that these paintings have any value, are you? They're not worth the canvasses they're painted on!"

By this point, with their eyes locked on one another, Holmes and Miss Adler were ignoring me completely. As they began circling one another, I took out my pencil and notebook, having seen this before, a kind of dance between the two of them in which they practically thought with one mind.

"Let us consider the history of art..." began Holmes, "...how our cave-dwelling ancestors took up some berries or pieces of charcoal and began to scrawl images of themselves and of various beasts on the walls of their homes..."

"...to somehow capture their experiences and their world..." continued Miss Adler.

"...perhaps to preserve an important memory or to simply mark the world with their presence..."

"...and consider that for millennia art has been largely representational..." went on Miss Adler.

"...just as with the cavemen, a product of the very human desire to record our own images, surroundings, and experiences," added Holmes.

"That desire still exists, so what has occurred in this century to cause such a radical departure from the representational tradition of painting?"

As one, Holmes and Miss Adler pronounced the single word, "Photography." And having cleared that deductive hurdle, their next words came in a rush.

"Of course!" began Holmes. "The invention of photography has made representational art completely unnecessary..."

"...as we can now record reality with a camera on photographic plates," added Miss Adler.

"Logically then, the art of painting should disappear completely because we no longer need it for its original purpose..."

"...but it hasn't disappeared because the desire to create still exists within us..."

"...and because it's not enough to simply record reality..."

"...we want to record our impression of reality..."

"...which is what these artists are striving to accomplish, all with very unique and individualistic styles never before seen in the art world."

"Quite beautifully reasoned, Mr. Holmes."

"Quite inspired by beauty, Miss Adler."

"I do love your mind..."

"As I love yours...and everything that surrounds it."

As fascinating as it could be to watch these back and forth exercises in deductive reasoning building to a crescendo, they often had the unfortunate effect of distracting Holmes and Miss Adler from the case at hand. Sure enough, a moment later Holmes and Miss Adler were engaged in a passionate embrace.

I like to think that it was on occasions such as these that the full value of my contribution to our consulting practice came to the fore. Beyond merely recording the cases for posterity and the delectation of the British reading public, I am proud to say that I was often the prime mover in getting cases back on track when things threatened to go off the rails completely, with Holmes and Miss Adler in danger of disappearing into a little universe of their own.

On some occasions this could be accomplished by little more than a cough or some forceful throat clearing, but in this instance it was clear that I was going to have to pull their attention back to the case in a more sustained fashion. Having done this many times before, I relied on a tried and true formula that had never failed me. First, there would be the compliments that they both secretly craved, followed by pointing out that questions remained and that the case was by no means cleared up, which served to stimulate their deductive and competitive instincts.

"I say," I began, "very well done! Yes indeed, beautifully reasoned! I see the chain...the links of the deductive chain that you two have forged and whatnot...quite brilliant...amazing, as a matter of fact...but if I may be so bold, you still haven't explained the—"

"The mystery!" Holmes exclaimed as he came up for air. "Why don't the paintings sell? Why are these artists unknown? Lack of exposure? An insufficient passage of time...?"

"Or is there a larger conspiracy afoot?" reasoned Miss Adler.

But before Holmes and Miss Adler could turn their considerable intellectual powers towards this conundrum, a sharp knock at the door interrupted the proceedings. Spotting Wilde's gloves on the back of the divan, I picked them up.

"Must be Wilde. Silly bugger's forgotten his gloves." I had already taken two steps towards the door when the expression on Miss Adler's face made me pause for a moment, and in that moment the penny dropped. "I didn't mean it that way! I just meant that he...he's forgotten his...I'll get the door."

But before I could move, I was brought up short by Holmes.

"Hold on, Watson. Let's not be hasty."

"Come now, Holmes," I remonstrated. "It's only Wilde."

"No, no. We have made some progress, but we are by no means on top of this case, and one can never be too careful," replied Holmes as he turned towards the door. "Who is it?"

"It's Wilde!" came the prompt answer, and I proceeded once more to the door.

"There. You see? Not every knock at the door announces the arrival of an assassin."

As I opened the door, Wilde strolled in with his typical flair, but for some reason holding his coat out as if he were a matador of some kind. Before I could quite make out the reason behind this rather peculiar behaviour, it became clear in a moment as Marie Chartier emerged from behind Wilde's coat, where she had rather cleverly concealed herself, and I could see that she had a gun firmly placed into the middle of Wilde's back. Having abandoned her widow's weeds, she was now attired in a quite striking green dress that suited her wonderfully, but I'm afraid that in the moment, I was more focused on the fact that I had quite literally allowed an assassin to enter our rooms.

"Oh dear," I heard myself saying. "Sorry, Holmes."

As was often the case, Miss Adler was there to buck me up when I got down on myself. "Now don't you blame yourself. It was a beautifully executed ruse."

While I always appreciated her kindness, the simple fact was that I had muffed it again, and I'm afraid that my exasperation was fairly evident to everyone in the room. Holmes, as ever, rose to the occasion.

"Steady on, old fellow. We'll soon have this sorted out. Miss Chartier! How delightful to see you again. And I gather that you've made the acquaintance of Mr. Wilde?"

"Oscar Wilde?" Miss Chartier was genuinely surprised. "The great writer and wit?"

"The same," replied Wilde, keeping his dignity as best as could be expected with the barrel of a gun pressing against his spine.

"I don't believe you."

"Believe what you like."

"Then say something witty."

"I will not."

"Why?"

From my vantage point I could see Wilde's jaw clench and it was evident that this was a sore spot for him.

"Because I am not some trained monkey who can be compelled to dance for your amusement! Have you any idea how grating it is, how insufferably agonising it is, that everywhere I go, every room I enter, some wag or another will shout out, 'Say something witty, Wilde!' Well no, I refuse."

"Something witty. Now."

"Absolutely not."

The unmistakable sound of a gun being cocked was heard by everyone in the room, and a look of panic flashed across Wilde's features.

"Um...the only thing I have to declare, is my genius!"

Miss Chartier regarded Wilde closely, the way a butterfly collector might regard a prize specimen before pinning it to a board.

"Again."

"Ah..." Wilde cast his eyes about the room. "Either this wallpaper goes, or I do!"

"Once more."

"Oh heavens...um..." Wilde was like an engine running out of steam, and I was beginning to rethink my theory that he had an endless store of witticisms at hand, at which point Miss Chartier took him out of his misery. Not with a bullet, thank goodness, but she proceeded to slam the butt of the gun against the back of Wilde's head, whereupon he tumbled senseless to the ground. It should have been shocking, but increasingly, it was becoming apparent that when it came to Miss Chartier, there was no way of predicting what she might say or do next.

"Perhaps I should have mentioned," she coolly explained, "I despise witty people."

"So it would appear," said Holmes. "Your medical bag, I think, Doctor."

I turned to go to my bedroom for my bag, but found myself staring down the barrel of Miss Chartier's gun. Having been in similar circumstances a few times over the course of the years, I can attest to the fact that it is never a pleasant experience, and on this occasion I was struck by the fact that the gun was absolutely rock-steady in Miss Chartier's hand.

"I think not. I would prefer if we all stayed in this room," she said.

"But you've knocked Wilde cold!" I pointed out.

"Indeed. You are particularly scintillating today, Dr. Watson." Miss Chartier turned to Holmes. "Is that how it is done? The snide condescension towards the one man in this world who is the closest thing you have to a friend?"

"When I say it, it's said with love and affection," returned Holmes. "And usually without a revolver shoved in his face."

Despite the gravity of the situation, I found my eyes sliding towards Holmes. I wanted to make certain that I had heard him correctly.

"Love? Do you mean that, Holmes?"

And as Holmes hesitated, it was Miss Adler who stepped in. "Oh, for God's sake. Yes, he does. Holmes loves you very much, Watson. He'd tell you himself, but he's too English."

Having Oscar Wilde unconscious on the floor and a gun pointed at my forehead by the most dangerous woman in Europe was bad enough, but now the situation had become decidedly awkward. Holmes and I had known one another for years, and during the course of that time we had uttered a few complimentary words back and forth of the "well done" and "nicely played" variety. More often, we both relied on glances of approval and small nods of our heads to indicate any particularly intense feelings of friendship and camaraderie. Having travelled fairly extensively, I was well aware that various cultures on the Continent conducted themselves much differently.

In France and Italy in particular, all manner of affectionate terms were commonplace, not to mention hugging and kissing between people who might have been perfect strangers only minutes previously. I have no means of proving this, but I suspect this is why an Englishman can get more done in a day that your typical Italian or Frenchman, who fawn all over one at another at the drop of a hat. The famous "stiff upper lip" of the Englishman is simply another way of saying that we get down to business and don't waste time on emotional histrionics of any kind.

Given all that, I never imagined that the word "love" would ever be uttered in any context between Holmes and myself, but here it was, and there was no denying it. I immediately put it down, of course, to the dubious influence of Miss Adler and the manner in which she had introduced a feminine perspective into our household. The idea of me replying in kind was simply unthinkable, and I could see a kind of wild terror in Holmes' eyes at the possibility that I might do just that. But then, to say nothing at all would be a bit rude and unfair to Holmes. Swallowing hard, I finally managed, "Oh...well, I'm rather fond of you too, old chap. In a rugged, manly way, of course!"

"Of course," said Holmes, and we exchanged a glance which fully communicated our mutual relief in having endured and escaped this particular ordeal.

I then became aware that I no longer had a gun pointed at my head and that Miss Chartier was strolling about the room looking at the various Post-Impressionist paintings we had scattered around. She regarded them thoughtfully, with what I would describe as a connoisseur's eye.

"You have been busy, I see. Quite the collection."

"You recognise the artists?" asked Miss Adler.

"Toulouse-Lautrec, Seurat, and Paul Gauguin, of course."

"Quite so...and your ready response is most suggestive."

"I concur," added Holmes, clearly pleased to be able to return his focus to the case. "So then, Miss Chartier, while entering a room with a drawn revolver is always an excellent way of getting everyone's attention, perhaps it would be simpler if you just told us what your game is."

This elicited a laugh from Miss Chartier. "My game, as you call it, is a very deep one, Mr. Holmes."

"And why is that? With your intelligence, beauty, and complete disregard for anyone save yourself, surely you have the world at your fingertips?"

I could see that Holmes was genuinely mystified, and as I considered Holmes' words, so was I. Miss Chartier was quite clearly a remarkable woman in every aspect. She had her father's brains, no scruples of any kind, and both of those singular traits were wrapped up in a physical package calculated to bring almost any man to his knees at the mere sight of her. Why then, this need for mystery and subterfuge to achieve her aims?

Miss Chartier simply responded with what sounded like a genuine sigh as she turned to Miss Adler. "He does not get it, does he?"

"Some days, yes. Some days, not so much."

I looked at Holmes, hoping for some kind of explanation for this kind of code that both women seemed to be speaking, but it was clear from his expression that he was as much at sea as I was. With an expression of infinite patience, Miss Chartier turned back to Holmes. "Being a criminal mastermind is difficult enough. Do you have any idea how hard it is being a female criminal mastermind?"

"I'm going to have to say 'no' on that."

"Well, Miss Adler here was a criminal mastermind—" I began.

"I blackmailed one king! Just one!" objected Miss Adler.

Holmes gazed at her admiringly, "And you were marvellous!"

Miss Chartier eyed Miss Adler. "Was it easy?"

"Manipulating men is always easy."

"True. But have you ever tried to build a criminal empire?"

"Can't say that I have."

I must say that I found this rather frank exchange between the two women unsettling in the extreme, like a child overhearing his parents talking about the cost of presents and expressing the wish that Father Christmas actually existed. The reality that I had always assumed to be true and permanent was beginning to dissolve in front of my very eyes with every word that Miss Adler and Miss Chartier uttered.

I could see that Holmes was disoriented as well, and I was overwhelmed by the conflicting urges to flee the room or to stay and witness the universe as I had known it shattered and then reformed into an entirely new configuration. Given the situation, there was nothing for it but to remain where I was and see how this played out, as Miss Chartier idly ran her finger along the frame of the Seurat and addressed Miss Adler.

"And there is the difference! Because here I am, as Mr. Holmes so perceptively observed—brilliant, ruthless, and beautiful. Not only that, I am the daughter of the celebrated Professor Moriarty, but do you think anyone in the world of organised crime would give me the time of day?"

"Wait just a moment. Are you saying that the Professor's organisation still exists?" Holmes' expression was one of complete incredulity.

"My father was only one man among many very special men...illuminated men, you might say."

"The Illuminati, of course!"

"The who?" I was still lost, but it was evident that Holmes was now back on familiar ground.

"The Illuminati, my dear fellow. A secret order founded over one hundred years ago in Bavaria. Devoted to absolute control over every aspect of civilised society by any means necessary. Their tendrils of influence pervade Europe and practically every country beyond, and their ultimate goal is a New World Order, with their members firmly in charge."

I don't believe I had ever heard a snort of contempt coming from a woman before, but I definitely heard the one that emerged from Miss Chartier.

"Pah! It is a glorified boys' club filled with greedy and ignorant men. Would they let me into the drug trade? No. Gambling? No. Steel, oil, finance? No. Carnegie, Rockefeller, and J. P. Morgan are, of course, exceptional criminals in their own way, but they all scoffed at the idea of allowing a woman into their enterprises. Every door was closed against me. And so at length, I resolved to carve my own path..."

"...into the world of art," concluded Miss Adler.

If I was confused before, now I felt that I had been ushered into a cell in Bedlam. The world of art? Yes, I understood perfectly well that vast fortunes could be accumulated in the various industries that Miss Chartier had named, and certainly paintings by masters like Da Vinci or Titian would fetch a pretty penny at an auction house. But as I looked around at the wild mélange of colours slathered on bits of canvas that Miss Adler had collected, I felt utterly cut adrift from reality.

"But these works of art are worthless!" I exclaimed. "The scruffy fellow taking up residence in my bedroom? He hasn't sold a single painting in his entire life! He's simply dreaming and deluding himself, not to mention taking advantage of his brother's kindness and generosity. I'm sorry, Miss Chartier, but if you are attempting to follow in your father's footsteps and to become a criminal genius, then I'm afraid I shall have to deem your little enterprise an abject failure on every level!"

I can't say that it was a good feeling speaking to a woman so forthrightly, but that was the plain and simple fact of the matter, and there was no point in pretending otherwise. To my surprise, Miss Chartier took my upbraiding in good stride.

"You may well laugh, Dr. Watson. My illuminated colleagues certainly did. They only see the profit that is under their very noses. I am playing, shall we say, a longer game."

"Which is?" asked Holmes.

"Oh no. That is the beauty of my game. No one can see it. Even you, Mr. Holmes, with all of your deductive skills, can only solve crimes that have already occurred. But the future? You are like a blind man in the fog. It would require a uniquely brilliant mind, in equal parts intelligent and possessed of a dazzling imagination, to glimpse even the shadow of my plan to—"

"—defraud and exploit artists!"

As one, we all turned to see that Oscar Wilde had regained consciousness and had decided to join the conversation.

Chapter Nine

The Van Gogh Collector

As Wilde slowly sat up, he rubbed the back of his head with a pained expression, and I was able to help him to his feet and get him into the armchair.

"That is the way it has always been," Wilde continued. "'I say Michelangelo, be a good chap and paint the Sistine Chapel, won't you? We can't pay you, but it will please God.' And today it's, 'I say Wilde, let us publish your poems. We can't pay you, but think of the exposure.' Miss Chartier, no doubt, has simply dreamt up a new version of an old song; specifically, the tune to which writers, artists, and composers starve to death in freezing garrets while the well-fed and warm upper-class enjoy all the delights of their genius. The neglect and disrespect that we heap upon those among us who wish to create beauty is, if I may so, one of the great travesties of humanity."

For different reasons, Wilde's words gave everyone in the room pause, and I could see a faint expression of concern on Miss Chartier's face.

"I must say, you have opened up a very suggestive line of enquiry, Mr. Wilde," said Holmes. "What say you, Miss Chartier?"

"I say that is quite enough small talk for me. Let me retrieve the item I came for, and I will be on my way."

For the life of me, I couldn't imagine what she was talking about. Had she come to burgle us? That scarcely seemed plausible, as neither Holmes, Miss Adler, nor I possessed anything of great value. Then I remembered that during her first visit, she had fired a shot at Holmes with the derringer pistol she had brought hidden in her purse, and had then tossed it aside in favour of a sword. That had to be it, and no doubt it was some sort of sentimental keepsake that had been passed down from her father to her. Looking about on the floor, I saw the gun peeking out from beneath the divan and went to retrieve it.

"You mean this?" I asked. "The little gun you left behind?"

"No. I mean my Van Gogh."

"Your...? What the devil are you talking about? We only had the one painting and you bloody well jumped out the window with it!"

"You misunderstand me, Dr. Watson. I want my Van Gogh. And I am not leaving here without him."

And with that, I once again found myself staring down the barrel of her gun.

"Watson, I suggest that you fetch Mr. Van Gogh from the bedroom," said Holmes. "He, apparently, is the item that Miss Chartier has come to collect."

With one wary eye on Miss Chartier, I quickly backed towards my bedroom door and rapped on it sharply, only to hear Van Gogh cry out, "Go away!"

Trying the doorknob, I was dismayed to find it locked, and so I knocked on the door again. "I say, Vince...Vinny, old man. Dr. Watson here. Could you possibly come out for a moment?"

"I said, go away! I must work!"

"You need to come out here this instant!"

"One reason! Give me one reason to come out! No! You do not have a reason, so I am not coming out!"

I could have barged the door down with my shoulder had I wished, but from experience I can tell you that while it is both spectacular and effective, it's a bit of a mess, inevitably a carpenter and locksmith need to be called in, and it's generally more trouble than it's worth, unless someone is well and truly in mortal peril. Happily enough, in this instance I knew I had a trump card that could be played, and so I played it.

"There's a woman here to see you!"

As I surmised, Van Gogh had no ready response to this. Instead, I heard the quick padding of footsteps, then the sound of the door being unlocked. It swung open and Van Gogh emerged, stopping in shock when he caught sight of Miss Chartier. She had put her gun behind her back and simply stood there, smiling slightly as she gazed at Van Gogh, the very image of innocent womanhood. Rooted to the spot, Van Gogh rubbed his eyes in disbelief, his face glowing with unholy joy.

"No...I have drunk too much absinthe! This can't be real...you're merely a vision...a phantom of my dreams..."

"And are they beautiful dreams, Vincent?"

"My God, ya!" Finally accepting that the vision in front of him was made of flesh and blood, Van Gogh took two rapid steps towards Miss Chartier, but as she held up a single finger, he stopped in his tracks.

"Were you given permission to approach?"

Confusion swept across Van Gogh's features. "No, but—"

"Or speak?"

Van Gogh shook his head, clearly at sea, but terrified of doing or saying the wrong thing.

"Then stay where you are," continued Miss Chartier, "or I will walk out of that door and you will never see me again."

"No!" It was a cry of the deepest despair that sprang from Van Gogh's throat. "No, please…"

All of this made one thing abundantly clear—Miss Chartier and Van Gogh were not strangers to one another. In fact, there was no question at all that Miss Chartier and Van Gogh's beloved Rachel were one and the same person. Years ago, I would have trumpeted this realisation to the heavens, declaring, "My God, Holmes, Miss Chartier is the *fille de joie* of Van Gogh!" only to be met with an expression of amused indulgence from Holmes.

Being a wiser man these days, I simply cast a quick look at Holmes, and his return glance from beneath hooded eyelids told me everything I needed to know. The only thing that was unclear at this point was whether or not Miss Chartier was aware that we had penetrated her alias, for she had no way of knowing precisely what Van Gogh had communicated to us.

As a pathetic whimper escaped Van Gogh, Miss Chartier put her finger to her lips, and at that Van Gogh fell silent. It was, in truth, a remarkable exhibition of the control that one human being can exert over another by sheer force of personality. To say that Van Gogh was smitten or infatuated with Miss Chartier would not come close to adequately describing the emotions that were practically tearing the poor man apart as he stood there.

In an instant, it was clear to me what the course of their relationship must have been. Van Gogh, as he had already noted, was not a wealthy, famous, or handsome man. Rather, as he had poetically expressed it, he had a great fire in his soul, but no one had ever come to warm themselves at it. I suspected that at some point, many years ago, during some dark night of the soul, he had bitterly concluded that he would never be genuinely loved by a woman.

He had thereupon poured every ounce of his passion into his art, until the day Miss Chartier had come along and recognised in him something that she coveted. Following that, she had played her part brilliantly. Van Gogh was known to be paranoid and mistrusting of strangers, so he would quite naturally have been suspicious if a beautiful and well-dressed lady had mysteriously appeared in the town of Arles and expressed interest in his art. He would have seen some kind of conspiracy at play and it would have been some time before she could gain his trust, if ever. Instead, Miss Chartier reinvented herself as the prostitute, Rachel, and had presented herself in that guise to Van Gogh.

After that, the unfortunate man had no chance. That she was beautiful and brilliant was incontestable. And she would have recognised instantly that the merest glance or touch from her would instantly cement Van Gogh's lifelong devotion. After all, he had quite willingly sliced off part of his own body for her, and I had no doubt that if she handed him a knife and ordered him to butcher himself for her amusement, he would do so with no hesitation whatsoever.

This was the pure, transcendent love so often praised and revered by poets down through the ages, but standing outside of it and seeing its effects, it was nothing less than terrifying and more than a little reminiscent of a serious mental illness.

"Impressive," commented Miss Adler, as she observed Van Gogh waiting at Miss Chartier's beck and call.

"I have found that not only can most men be trained..." for some reason Miss Chartier's gaze had wandered towards me, "...they want to be trained."

With that, she raised one perfect eyebrow and for a moment I could feel a bottomless abyss opening up before me. Thankfully, my training as a soldier and English gentleman served me in good stead, and I was able to manage a dismissive snort. Unfortunately, Miss Chartier took that as a challenge.

"Would you not agree, Dr. Watson?"

As she came towards me, I was inexorably reminded of a panther on the prowl, and I felt my mouth going dry and my heart thumping against my ribs like a trapped animal.

"No!" I managed. "Nonsense! You're talking absolute—"

And it was at that precise moment that Miss Chartier took me by the lapels, pulled me towards her, and kissed me long and hard. It could not have lasted more than five seconds, but I feel quite certain that to adequately describe those five seconds would take me several volumes. I also know, that since that moment, not a day has passed that I haven't thought about that kiss.

I should, of course, not even be discussing this, and were this story intended for my typical "Strand" reader, the incident would never be mentioned at all. Still, I imagine that my philosopher friend Jean-Jacques Rousseau would want me to be honest with both myself and my reader, so I shall make some feeble effort to recount the lifetime that I experienced in that all too brief moment.

First, there was the shock of her very real physical strength. I am not, by any means, an insubstantial man, and it's entirely conceivable that my Christmas diet had added more than a few pounds to my already ample frame. Still, when she pulled me towards her, I moved, and not of my own volition. She then paused for a moment, looking into my eyes, and in that moment I could feel the warmth of her body, smell the sandalwood notes in her perfume, and feel her breath mingling with my own. It was beyond intoxicating, and I felt my willpower evaporating beneath her measured gaze.

The kiss itself was warm and honey-like, soft and yet assertive, a gesture of intimacy to be sure, but also a gesture of one animal asserting its dominance over another. When she released me, I finally formed an understanding of what the expression "weak in the knees" really means. I felt thoroughly, beautifully, and calculatingly assaulted, and as I found myself falling back onto the divan and gazing up at her, I was possessed of no feeling or desire other than to be assaulted like that for the remainder of eternity.

Through my haze, I heard Miss Adler saying, "You're quite the specimen, Miss Chartier. Or should I say...Rachel?"

Miss Chartier wasn't fazed in the least to hear her Arles alias said out loud. "Allow me to return the compliment, Mrs. Hudson. Or should I say... Irene?"

This brief exchange was like a bucket of cold water to my addled senses. How on earth had Miss Chartier seen through Miss Adler's alias? Reading both my expression and my mind, Holmes spared me the embarrassment of asking the question out loud.

"Oh, there's no mystery there, Watson. Shortly after Miss Chartier returned, you became a shade excited when she lamented the difficulties inherent in being a criminal of the female persuasion, at which point you referred to Irene as 'Miss Adler' and proclaimed her to be a criminal mastermind thanks to her blackmailing scheme involving the King of Bohemia. Don't you recall?"

Dimly, I remembered saying something about someone at some point, but the events of the past few minutes had rendered my memory a bit hazy and unreliable.

Thankfully, I never had to answer Holmes' question, as to my considerable astonishment, I observed Oscar Wilde creeping up behind Miss Chartier. Having quite sensibly determined that Holmes and Miss Adler were the most obvious threats in the room, she had positioned herself to keep an eye on both of them, with her gun at the ready if needed. Showing more pluck than I would have given him credit for, Wilde silently approached Miss Chartier, and with a swift motion snatched the gun from her hand.

"Well, well, well!" crowed Wilde. "What an unexpectedly delightful turn of events, Miss Chartier! So it is in the guise of Rachel that you live the poetry you cannot write."

Miss Chartier immediately wheeled on Van Gogh, her eyes flashing. "What stories have you been telling about me?"

"Nothing! I love you, Rachel!"

"Which is why you mutilated yourself? To prove your love?"

"Ya! Ya!!!"

"And your ear was to be a gift to me? So where is it?"

"I don't know!" Van Gogh was in agony at his predicament. "That is why I came here, to Mr. Holmes. He will help me find it!" Van Gogh turned to Holmes. "You must!"

With Miss Chartier disarmed, Holmes finally had time to consider the situation in all of its strange and apparently disconnected facets. This, of course, is where he excelled as a consulting detective. His deep knowledge of crime and extraordinarily retentive memory allowed him to see patterns where there only appeared to be chaos to any random observer. Bit by bit, and piece by piece, he would collect odd scraps of information to fill in the parts of a puzzle that only he could see.

This, of course, is where his pipe smoking became invaluable. The process of retrieving the pipe, filling it, tamping down the tobacco, lighting it, and then taking a meditative puff, gave him sufficient time to organise his thoughts and closely consider the next thing that he would say. On this occasion, he opted for his blackened clay pipe, and it was only as the first puffs of smoke made their way towards the ceiling that Holmes turned back to Van Gogh.

"Well, perhaps I have a notion or two regarding the whereabouts of your severed ear. But first, let us fill in some of the missing pieces to this puzzle. For example, you never told us what happened after you cut your ear off."

"I'm not certain..." began Van Gogh hesitantly. "I think I lost consciousness. I must have. When I awoke I searched the ground around me, but could find nothing..."

"And so you suspect that—"

"It was Paul! It must have been! He was jealous of my love for Rachel. He knew he could never equal it, and so he took my ear away with him so that I could not give it to her! And I know where he has gone! The South Seas! That is all that he could talk about once he had a glass or two of absinthe in him. He's probably halfway there by now!"

Finally, I felt that I could see what this case was all about and why Van Gogh had come to London in the first place. "So that's why you came here? To have Holmes track down this Gauguin fellow and recover your missing ear? You want Holmes to go to the South Seas?"

"Ya!" Van Gogh was as happy as a toddler who has finally succeeded in making himself understood by the adults in the room.

"But that's impossible!" I objected. "Polynesia has over one thousand islands! You can't very well expect Holmes to visit each one and simply start asking around! 'Excuse me, have you seen a French artist with a Dutch artist's ear?' It's preposterous!"

"Not necessarily all that preposterous, Watson," opined Wilde. "Many of the islands are uninhabited, and it's no secret that when he was frequenting the cafés of Paris, Gauguin often expressed the fervent desire to visit one of those islands in particular; namely, Tahiti. If, in fact, he has fled Europe, I don't doubt that is where you will find him."

"Will you do it, Mr. Holmes?" pleaded Van Gogh. "Will you go to Tahiti and find Gauguin? I will go with you, if you wish."

"Well, I would do that, Mr. Van Gogh," replied Holmes, "and I would do that quite happily, because I know that there is nothing of more value in this world than love."

"Indeed," added Wilde. "One should always be in love, which is why one should never get married."

Damn it all. He was good. Dimly, I began to realise that no matter how many hours I might spend conjuring up witticisms for every occasion, I would never be as quick or witty as Wilde. However, before I could venture further down this dark path of resentful jealousy, I realised that Holmes had taken up a central position in the room with his eyes fixed on the ceiling. In addition to his detecting abilities, Holmes was an inveterate actor, and this was what might be termed his spotlight pose.

It invariably meant that a villain was about to be exposed or an object was about to be found, and so I sat with my pencil ready, anxious to get every word and gesture precisely. If I couldn't be Oscar Wilde, I knew beyond certainty that I could be John Watson, and that is the task to which I would dedicate whatever meagre abilities I possessed.

Taking a meditative puff on his pipe, Holmes watched the smoke drift upward, apparently reading within it the answers to the mysteries surrounding us. "However, before we set sail for Tahiti to enjoy all of the delights that the island surely holds, I do feel obliged to note that there is one problem with your lurid tale of self-mutilation, Mr. Van Gogh," Holmes began, "and I'm afraid that it's a rather significant problem."

"What?" Van Gogh's expression was one of utter perplexity. "What do you mean?"

"What I mean is that your tale is nothing more than that...a tale."

Van Gogh cast a panicky look at Miss Chartier, then fell to his knees before Holmes. "No, Mr. Holmes! I assure you that what I have said is true. You must believe me!"

"But I don't." This was Holmes at his imperious best. Somehow, he was now in possession of information unknown to anyone else. Whatever mysterious fog there might have been throughout the case, it had now been swept aside by the cool wind of his implacable logic. Like a locomotive gaining speed, he was now thundering down the track, and woe to anyone who stood in his way. Even Van Gogh seemed to sense the terrible inevitability that was approaching, and yet he still kept protesting.

"You saw for yourself! The lower part of my ear is missing!"

"Indeed it is, but through no contrivance or action of your own." Finally, Holmes deigned to look down at Van Gogh. "Get up, man. There's no use snivelling on your knees and repeating the same lie over and over."

Slowly, Van Gogh struggled to his feet. When he worked up the courage to look at Holmes, it was with the eyes of a condemned man staring at the blade of the guillotine.

"Let us reconstruct the scenario, shall we?" continued Holmes. "I will repeat the very actions you performed in this room just a short while ago. You say that you and Gauguin were quarrelling, and I have no doubt that copious amounts of absinthe were involved. Logic dictates that the dispute, in fact, began in a café. Your confrontation then spilled out into the street, where things became more and more heated. The point of contention, of course, was Miss Chartier, or rather, Rachel, as she was known in Arles. Everything was going according to her plan. Having heard about your dubious reputation in Paris and seen your work at your brother Theo's gallery, she followed you to Arles to, shall we say, make your acquaintance.

"This was speedily accomplished, and with her hook firmly set and her grand scheme slowly taking shape, she then suggested that you invite Paul Gauguin to live with you. You immediately complied, as you would have complied if she had told you to adopt a troop of baboons. There was nothing that you would not do for her. Upon Mr. Gauguin's arrival, he was similarly swept into her net, both of you now doing anything, saying anything, and painting anything to gain her favour and attention. And so things came to a head, as she knew they would. The battle between you and Gauguin was finally joined in earnest. Insults were hurled, your passion and anger blazing up inside you, and it was at that point, Mr. Van Gogh, that you expect us to believe that you severed your own ear with a razor."

"Which I did!"

"No. For what manner of man carries a razor with him to a café? You then proceeded to show us how you committed the deed." Here, Holmes removed a sword from amongst our fireplace tools and precisely mimicked Van Gogh's earlier demonstration. "You raised your left hand as one would to grasp and steady the lobe of the left ear, then sliced through the ear from back to front."

"Ya! Ya, that is precisely what happened!"

"Again no. First, you are left-handed and would naturally hold the razor in that hand. Second, such a wound would be lateral in nature, as one would instinctively wish to avoid the fingers securing the earlobe. Your wound is at a pronounced angle, from high in the back to low in the front."

Here Holmes paused to gaze around the room, gauging the effect that his recitation was having on his listeners. Miss Adler's eyes were shining, her lips slightly parted, and I knew from past experience that if she could have her way in that moment, she would have bundled Holmes off to the bedroom in a heartbeat. Wilde was absolutely transfixed, one storyteller recognising the genius of another storyteller, while at the same time gauging what parts of Holmes' speech he could adapt into a tale or two of his own. For her part, Miss Chartier had an altogether different expression as she gazed from Holmes to Van Gogh.

For some time now Van Gogh had been her marionette, a kind of plaything that she could pick up or discard on a whim. As Holmes had rightfully said, if she could be certain of one thing, it was that he would do as he was told and say what he was told to say. But now, thanks to Holmes' recitation, it was becoming more and more clear that the marionette had somehow slipped his strings and taken on a life of his own.

Van Gogh was clearly aware of the very same thing, and the look he cast at Miss Chartier was one of fear and terror. Turning back to Holmes, he clutched his hands together in prayer.

"No, please! I beg you!"

However, all of his pleading was to no effect. The locomotive was almost upon him, as in dramatically slow motion, Holmes swung the sword towards Van Gogh, stopping just short of the bloody wound hidden by the bandage.

"All of which can mean only one thing—your ear was severed by Paul Gauguin!"

"No!!!" Van Gogh's wrenching cry must surely have been heard two blocks away.

But Holmes was unmoved, pressing home his point relentlessly. "A man whom, as we just learned from Mr. Wilde, just happens to be an adept swordsman. Your bizarre story of self-mutilation? It served two purposes: to keep a man you admire out of trouble with the law, and to convince your beloved Rachel that you would do virtually anything to prove your devotion to her. It was, in truth, a beautifully constructed fiction that would no doubt fool almost anyone who heard it, and quite in keeping with your previous instances of eccentric behaviour and lapses in social decorum. Your only mistake was coming here and presenting it to me."

It was in moments like these that my heart swelled with pride at simply knowing Holmes. It is one thing to read the world, to take in factual information and see a chain of events logically unfolding. However, it is when you add human beings to the equation—scheming, posing, lying human beings—that the truth can become a kind of will 'o the wisp that is forever elusive and out of reach, because while we like to tell ourselves that we want to hear the truth, the reality is that we are far more desirous of the truths we want to hear. We practically advertise our desire to be lied to on a constant basis, whether it's a politician promising the moon or a health tonic promising to cure all of our ills.

Tall tales, elaborate ruses, and outright fabrications are the stuff of which modern society is composed, except for those rare individuals like Sherlock Holmes. I sincerely believe that it is this quality, more than any other, that made Holmes a hero to so many of his readers, and I will readily confess I was not immune to its power myself, as on this occasion I found myself blurting out, "Bravo, Holmes! Wonderfully deduced!" By no means immune to praise, Holmes acknowledged my effusive admiration with a small tilt of his head.

As for Mr. Van Gogh, it was clear that the combination of absinthe overindulgence, the appearance of his beloved Rachel, and Holmes' accusations had effectively demolished any pretences that he may have had when he came to us for help. He was now staggering about the room, wrapped in remorse and self-pity, humiliated in front of the woman he loved, with tears running down his face. "It's true, all true...I'm a liar...God help me, I'm a liar..."

And with that, Van Gogh fainted dead away.

I felt a slight nudge at my elbow and found Miss Adler looking at me. "Dr. Watson, perhaps your medical bag...?"

"Yes, of course!"

I hustled quickly into my bedroom, opened up my bag to verify that I had some smelling salts, and then was back in time to see Marie Chartier nudging Van Gogh's inert form with her boot, a small smile playing on her lips.

"Poor Vincent. When he said that he was coming to London to consult you, I knew I had to follow him to make certain he did not disrupt my little enterprise. And now it has come to this...dear me."

Making herself quite at home, Miss Chartier moved to the sideboard and poured herself a sherry. If nothing else, I must admit that I admired her incredible composure. Taking a small sip, she smiled at us.

"Why are you so pleased with yourself?" asked Miss Adler.

"It is always pleasing to see one's plans coming to fruition."

"Feeding on the misery of a poor artist?" Wilde chimed in. "What kind of monster are you? Can't you do something, Mr. Holmes?"

By all rights, as a physician, I should have been endeavouring to bring Van Gogh back to consciousness by the judicious use of smelling salts, but when I saw that Holmes was about to speak, I brought out my notebook instead. Van Gogh would awaken soon enough on his own, and I didn't want to miss a word of what Holmes was about to say.

"Perhaps to an extent," began Holmes. "I don't imagine that I can convince Mr. Van Gogh to see Miss Chartier for what she really is, for he is a man in love. On the other hand, let us see if we can begin to unravel Miss Chartier's scheme just a bit. So, what are the facts currently in our possession? She is, or at least claims to be, the daughter of the late Professor Moriarty. Judging by her intellect, inclination towards crime, and general physiognomy, I see no point in challenging that assertion.

"I believe that she is who she claims to be. In attempting to follow in her father's footsteps, she is not content with petty crimes, but instead feels that it is almost her birthright to embark upon an extraordinarily ambitious scheme that no one before her has attempted or even imagined. It is, I daresay, utterly audacious in its scope. To that end, and as her first step, she attached herself to a struggling artist..."

"...but is his life really all that different from that of Seurat, Lautrec, or Gauguin?" interjected Miss Adler.

We all turned to Wilde for his opinion, and he did not disappoint. "Not particularly. They are all poor, largely unrecognised, with chaotic personal lives, and assorted addictions."

"In other words," continued Holmes, "not particularly promising material if one is proposing to establish a criminal empire. However, it wouldn't do to stop there. We must give Miss Chartier credit that she knows what she's doing. She is, after all, her father's daughter. Where others see nothing, she sees opportunity, and that is clearly what she saw when she looked at these men. What manner of opportunity? Ah, there is the question of the moment, because these artists have absolutely nothing to offer her in the way of money, status, or connections.

"And yet, there is something that all of them share, a common bond, as it were. And that is nothing more and nothing less than their complete and utter devotion to their art. All of these men could make do in other fields; in fact, as Mr. Wilde just related to us, Paul Gauguin was once a stockbroker. They could get by as so many people do, with a job to pay the bills, a spouse who grows increasingly indifferent with the passing years, and children whose adulthood never quite matches the promise of their youth.

"They could bundle away their hopes and dreams into some dusty corner of their hearts and proceed to lead very quiet, very sensible, and very anonymous lives. But no. Each of these men has turned his back on that kind of life to focus on his art..."

"To an obsessive degree," added Miss Adler.

"And here, we cannot allow ourselves to be led astray," continued Holmes. "We must resist the temptation to focus only on the aesthetic quality of these paintings. For beauty, as we all know, is in the eye of the beholder, and any new form of music, literature, or art is likely to be held in contempt during the first years of its existence. Such are the barriers thrown up by the supposed gatekeepers of culture. The patina of age is generally required before a new art form suddenly becomes revered and respected.

"In addition, these paintings are not meant to be representational in any conventional sense of the word, so who knows what sort of image or scene will appeal to a prospective buyer or collector? If we therefore take the next logical step and decide to spare ourselves the effort of judging the artistic quality of these works, then we may agree that what we are gazing upon is little more than smudges of colours on canvas. So, where is the value? The profit? I put it to you that it is not in the paintings themselves."

As rapt as my attention had been, I felt that Holmes had clearly lost the place, so to speak. The appeal and value of a painting has nothing to do with the painting itself? That made absolutely no sense to me, but judging from the expression on Miss Adler's face, she didn't share my concern or confusion.

"Oh yes, sweetheart," she began. "That's it! That must be it!"

"Quite right," Wilde was nodding his agreement. "Well done, Mr. Holmes! I do believe you have the cracked the code to Miss Chartier's grand scheme."

"Wonderful!" I found myself saying. "Splendid! Now if one of you could please explain to me what I am apparently missing, I would be most grateful!"

It was Miss Adler who took pity on me, "It's just as Holmes says. It's not the paintings themselves that have value, it is the artists who have value, or more specifically, their stories. It is their tortured, unhappy, miserable lives that will make their paintings almost priceless in the very near future."

"Because these painters possess precisely what upper-class, wealthy collectors want," added Wilde, "the one thing they can't buy—an authentic life free of the compromises and pathetic façades that must be endured to maintain reputation and status. These artists may be poor, miserable, and unrecognised, but they are free. They are pursuing a dream at the expense of a well-fed bourgeois existence. They are, I daresay, heroic in a way that no soldier, adventurer, or explorer can ever be heroic. They are the heroes of truth and beauty. The heroes of the human soul."

And with that, I am happy to say, the scales finally dropped from my eyes. Surely that was it. How Holmes had managed to discern this now self-evident truth was utterly beyond me, but in a moment all of the separate pieces of the puzzle had settled into place to reveal Miss Chartier's scheme in its entirety. And when I turned to look at her, expecting to see shock or horror at being exposed, I saw nothing of the kind. Instead, she was regarding us all with a bemused smile and clapping silently.

Chapter Ten
The Larger Picture

"*Salut!* It is a pleasure meeting such refined people as yourselves," began Miss Chartier as she looked down at the unconscious form of Van Gogh. "Yes, Vincent here is a pet project of mine. I first heard of him in Paris, and all that the other artists could speak of was his temper and wild mood swings. The more they talked the more fanciful the tales became—that he heard voices, that he would have fits in which he ate his own paint, and that he was in and out of asylums. Even before I met him, he had assumed this almost legendary status, and all this about a man who had yet to sell a single painting.

"And so when I heard that he had moved down to Arles in the south of France, I moved there as well—the huntress pursuing her prey, as it were. It was an easy thing to make his acquaintance. He had no friends there and I like to think that I am possessed of certain charms. In fact, I will flatter myself and tell you that within an hour of meeting him, Vincent was a devoted slave to me and would do anything that I desired. His passion is indeed without bounds. When he loves, it is with a purity I have never encountered in anyone else.

"And so I would send him out day after day, night after night into the fields and the town with only the single instruction, 'Paint me something beautiful, Vincent.' And that is precisely what he does. Yes, we would receive letters from his brother Theo on occasion, asking Vincent to send him work, and so I made certain that he sends only his weakest paintings to his brother, while I keep the rest. I was interested to see what kind

137

of effect the presence of Paul Gauguin would have on Vincent, and I must say that the results were most gratifying.

"Day after day they would compete for my attention, like two rutting rams in the mountains, and I could practically hear their horns crashing into one another with each painting that they brought to me for my approval. As for the other Post-Impressionists, Seurat and Lautrec, for example, when any of their work raises a serious ripple of interest, I simply have my agents take it off the market. So there. What of it? I am merely an art speculator. Perhaps I will succeed in making a small profit, but then again, perhaps not."

Put that way, I must say that it all seemed perfectly plausible. I felt bad for Van Gogh, of course, being controlled and manipulated by a jezebel as cold and heartless as Marie Chartier, but he would scarcely be the first man in history to debase and ruin himself for the sake of a woman. Still, for all of her machinations, it struck me that her efforts would end up being an enormous waste of time. Who on earth would want a fuzzy mass of random colours on their wall simply because it was painted by an addict or a madman?

"Quite a pretty little tale," I heard Miss Adler saying. "But it won't do, Miss Chartier. You are your father's daughter and your scheme is much grander than you pretend. In fact, I begin to see the form of a larger, darker web taking shape..."

"I do not know what you can mean," replied Miss Chartier.

"The problem with most of our lives," continued Miss Adler, "is that we are consumed with the present. What should we wear today? What shall we have for lunch? Should we pay that bill tomorrow or next week? When we are children, we delight in the world and all of its possibilities, but as we grow older those possibilities shrink down week by week and year by year.

"We trudge back and forth along the same path day after day, our view of the world getting narrower and narrower, until finally we are trudging in a trench of our own making and that is all we can see before us until the trench collapses and we are buried in the decomposing remains of our hopes and dreams. But not you, Miss Chartier. Not you. As your father's child you have lived your life on a razor's edge, always alert for catastrophe and the sound of the hounds upon your trail. You have your nose in the wind, and you sense changes in that wind long before other people. And it was just such a change that caused you to embark upon your current breathtakingly bold and prescient enterprise."

As Miss Adler spoke, I could see the muscles in Miss Chartier's jaw tightening. Even Holmes and Wilde were staring at Miss Adler, their eyes sparkling in anticipation at what she might say next. Genius recognises genius, as it were, and Miss Adler knew very well that she had the room in the palm of her hand. Van Gogh was still on the floor, his shallow breathing the only indication that he was still alive, as Miss Adler resumed.

"Like everything else in this age, the world of art and culture is changing before our very eyes thanks to industry and technology. One by one, the artisans of the world are disappearing, one by one the bookbinders and shoemakers close up their shops with no one to replace them, and there is no need to replace them. Mass production and distribution have become the holy grail of industry. To produce more and more for less and less is the dream of every entrepreneur and businessman.

"Everything is cheaper and more temporary. We no longer fix, repair, or cherish, no, we simply discard, and we are becoming a society whose profits are predicated upon waste. Something that is thrown out must be replaced, and it is invariably replaced by something even cheaper and shoddier that will need to be replaced even sooner.

"And what happens when that mentality is applied to the world of art? What happens when a book, a painting, or a symphony is no longer cherished for its beauty, but is simply another commodity? The popular yellow-back novels that people read on the train are so flimsy and worthless they are often simply left behind for other passengers and they practically disintegrate after a dozen readings. Any work of art by Raphael or Botticelli can now be copied and sold for pennies in an alley.

"And with Mr. Edison's invention of the phonograph, a symphony by Mozart or Beethoven can be recorded and played over and over. That is the future that Miss Chartier has foreseen, and she knows quite well that the day is coming when people will expect their art, their literature, and their music to be virtually free, with no compensation for the artists themselves. And so, the only form of art that will have any value at all will be..."

Miss Adler let her final words hang dramatically in the air. It was, quite naturally, Holmes who picked up the thread.

"Originals. A first edition of a book, a live performance by a musician, or in the case of the Post-Impressionists, an original painting from the tortured hand of the artist himself."

"*Très bien!*" Miss Chartier had recovered her equilibrium. "And please be so kind as to remind me, what is the best part of my little enterprise, the *coup de grâce*, if you will?"

"No crime is actually being committed," said Wilde. "Damn you to hell."

Miss Chartier flashed Wilde her most winning smile. "And I look forward to being welcomed to the warmer regions by you, my dear Oscar."

It was at that moment that I heard a soft groan from Van Gogh and looked down to see him stirring on the floor. He looked around for a moment with unseeing eyes, and I managed to help him sit up. "There we are, old chap! You just rest a moment, eh? Let's just get you a bit more comfortable."

I didn't want to risk standing him up and having him lose consciousness again, so I gently maneuvered him so that he was able to rest against the divan. In an instant, Miss Chartier was sitting on the divan near him and had taken Van Gogh's hand. Suddenly, the rapacious harpy version of Marie Chartier was gone, and was instantly replaced by our very own Florence Nightingale. "Oh, my poor Vincent! So it was Paul who did this terrible thing to you? The beast!"

Her transformation from conniving villain to doting lover fooled no one in the room but Van Gogh, and of course, he was the only one she needed to fool. When he looked up at her, it was with the adoring eyes of a man gazing upon a goddess.

"I am sorry, my love! I could apologise to you from now until the end of time and it would not be enough. But Gauguin was saying such horrible things...that you were a scheming whore...the Devil incarnate..."

"...and so you protected my honour? And the coward struck you with his sword? My poor, brave Vincent!"

Van Gogh rested his head in her lap, and as she stroked his hair he poured out his heart to her. "Ya. But then, I didn't want Paul to be arrested, so I made up that stupid, shameful lie about mutilating myself to prove my love to you...as if any woman would want the severed ear of her lover."

"Oh, but I would, Vincent. I want anything and everything that you can give me. Your art, your love, everything."

"Even...?"

"I would give several worlds for your severed ear as proof of your love."

That was a bit much, and I felt that I couldn't simply stand by and watch this black widow of a woman wind poor Van Gogh any tighter within her web. "Oh, for God's sake! That's laying it on a bit thick, don't you think? She's playing you for a fool!"

"Rachel? No! If she wants my ear, then she must have it!" Van Gogh turned to Holmes. "Mr. Holmes, I beseech you! I came here for your help. Please...can you exert all of your powers on my behalf?"

"I don't see why not." Holmes gazed around at the assembled faces, and I could tell he was about to launch into another one of his deductive speeches. I had absolutely no clue what he was about to say, and I wanted to hear it more than anyone, but in that moment what came rushing upon me was the simple fact that for all of the fascinating and bizarre details of this case, not one of them had improved the state of our bank account by so much as a single farthing.

And so, like a rude audience member who interrupts the conductor the moment he raises his baton, I strode to the middle of the room, arms waving, and fairly forced Holmes back into his armchair.

"No! I'm sorry, we're not doing that! No complimentary ear-finding will be taking place! This is a professional agency and professional services must be paid for!"

"But I brought you a painting!" objected Van Gogh.

"Which Miss Chartier stole!" I replied, establishing quite firmly that Holmes and Miss Adler weren't the only ones in the room capable of applying implacable logic. Of course, I hadn't counted on the sinuous charm of Miss Chartier, which seemingly enabled her to extricate herself from almost any difficult position.

"I am sorry, Vincent," she began, "but it is the only painting in the world with both of us in it. I could not bear anyone but me having your work."

"And that's another lie!" I fairly shouted. "Just like the one about wanting your ear!"

"But I do want it! I swear! More than anything!" Miss Chartier kept up her pose wonderfully for Van Gogh's sake, but when she looked at me it was with a wink and a small smile. Incredibly, despite all of the evidence on my side, I began to realise that I was fighting a losing battle. If forced to choose whom to believe, me or Miss Chartier, Van Gogh wouldn't give it a second thought. Desperate, I turned to Wilde.

"Wilde, for God's sake, say something! Tell him that she's Satan in the flesh!"

"Not at all," replied Wilde. "It is absurd to divide people into good and bad. People are either charming or tedious, but it is true that there is nothing quite so tedious as the desire to profit from the genius and labor of others."

For whatever reason, Wilde's words seemed to resonate within Van Gogh. Perhaps it was the memory of Miss Chartier's flirtation with Gauguin, or perhaps there was another incident or two that cast a shadow of doubt in his mind, but as Van Gogh gazed upon her now, it wasn't so much adoration in his eyes as a question. Keenly aware that her position was possibly becoming a bit tenuous, Miss Chartier rose to the occasion magnificently.

"Very well. Since my words are being called into question, let my actions speak for themselves. You say this is a professional agency? Then I hereby commission you, Mr. Holmes, to recover Vincent's ear. I will pay one thousand pounds for its return."

And with that, Miss Chartier reached into her bodice and removed the thick roll of notes that she had brought earlier and handed it to Holmes.

That was all it took. In an instant, Van Gogh was more ensnared in her web than he had ever been. "Rachel! My darling! I knew it! You do love me!"

"Of course," Miss Chartier continued, "should you fail to find it, Mr. Holmes, I would expect my money to be returned."

"You cunning devil!" I said. "That's what you're counting on, isn't it? That the ear was gobbled up by some mongrel in the streets of Arles and you've given Holmes an impossible task!"

"Have I?" Miss Chartier was vastly amused by the predicament in which she had now placed Holmes. It was maddening, but it appeared that there was nothing that any of us could do. However, when I looked at Holmes, he didn't appear to be distressed or bothered in the least. Instead, he got to his feet and began idly thumbing through the pound notes, apparently counting them to verify that it was indeed a thousand pounds, before flickering a glance at me and clearly perceiving my frustration.

"Steady, Watson. This case has included a number of remarkable elements, but from the outset, it was apparent that there was larger game afoot. I was most struck by Mr. Van Gogh's insistence that he had severed his own ear, when a single glance told me that was not the case. Why should a man tell such a tale? What other forces were operating behind the scenes? Mr. Van Gogh's ear was merely the smallest piece of the puzzle."

"But where is it?" asked Van Gogh. "Is it with Paul? Did he take it with him to the South Seas? Or is it still somewhere in the dust of Arles?"

Holmes clasped his hands behind his back and raised his gaze to the ceiling.

"No, Mr. Van Gogh. Your ear is in this very room."

Van Gogh visibly flinched at Holmes' words, "Please, sir. I am in a fragile enough state as it is. Don't play with my emotions."

"I wouldn't dream of it." Holmes looked Van Gogh up and down. "From the moment you arrived, it was evident that you are a man drawn to bright and vibrant colours. Witness especially the festive shades of yellow and blue that adorn your jacket in a number of places. And yet, I immediately detected another hue upon your clothing, a deep burgundy red in a rather singular location. Blood, Mr. Van Gogh, which told me at a glance that your ear has never left you. Indeed, your missing auditory appendage is in the cuff of your trousers, where it fell after you were struck by Paul Gauguin!"

Disbelieving, and scarcely daring to look, Van Gogh reached into the cuff of his trousers, his fingers fumbling, until with a cry of guttural joy he held his severed ear aloft for all to see, before turning to Miss Chartier.

"There! You see? Here it is! It is my gift to you, my sweet! My love! My everything!"

The pure happiness radiating from Van Gogh's countenance was a nice contrast to Miss Chartier's complexion, which had gone a few shades whiter. In the totality of her grand scheme, she had surely accounted for any number of possible scenarios, but she could have scarcely planned for this—the fact that Van Gogh's ear would be severed in the streets of Arles and that it would be recovered at 221B Baker Street in London. Still, to her credit, she forced a smile upon her face and beckoned Van Gogh towards her. She held out her hand, and Van Gogh, holding his grisly trophy aloft, gently placed it in her palm as if it were the most delicate flower on earth.

That, I am happy to say, was not the only transaction that took place, as Holmes approached me holding out the thousand pounds.

"And since this case began with your concerns regarding our finances, this, my dear Watson, now belongs to you."

As Holmes placed the money in my palm, Wilde and Miss Adler applauded, and I couldn't resist a look of triumph in the direction of Miss Chartier.

"Well done, Mr. Holmes!" cried Wilde. "Bravo! I had always imagined that Watson here had exaggerated your abilities to a certain degree, but I can see that I was mistaken. Quite brilliant! I feel that I have just witnessed a true artist at work! Well done, sir!"

And as Holmes bowed in Wilde's direction, Miss Chartier managed to drag her gaze from the severed ear in her hand to cast a withering look at Holmes.

"Yes. Well done, indeed."

With Van Gogh's ear recovered, I knew that Holmes would rapidly lose interest in the case, so I felt it was up to me to wrap up affairs in an appropriate manner.

"I say, Holmes," I began, "shall I conclude the case by contacting Inspector Lestrade to come and arrest Miss Chartier?"

"Arrest me for what, precisely?" asked Miss Chartier.

"Well, you...there's the...hang on a moment...oh, you stole our painting!"

"Since I am in the portrait, Vincent had no right giving it away without my permission."

"All right, fine!" I agreed. "But you tried to kill Holmes!"

"Did I? You seem to have a number of bullet holes in your wall. I was simply contributing to your somewhat eccentric decor, although I see that you never did finish the letter 'V' in 'V R.' Let me have my gun and I will tidy that up for you."

Miss Chartier approached Wilde, who I was alarmed to see did not do the sensible thing and back away. Instead, flush with the triumph of the moment, he made the decision to taunt Miss Chartier by holding her gun out towards her.

"As I like to say, Miss Chartier, there are only two tragedies in life. One is getting what you want..." Miss Chartier reached for the gun and Wilde pulled it away, "...and the other is not getting it. That's actually much wittier the other way around, but you get my point."

Wilde was absolutely delighted with himself, but he had made a fatal miscalculation. For all of his genius, like any of us, his experiences with human beings over time had led him to develop certain expectations. In the streets of London, at his favourite restaurant, or at the Albemarle club, the steady ebb and flow of human exchanges fell within fairly well-established parameters. In this instance, what he neglected to take into account was that Miss Chartier was not like most other people.

Beyond her pleasing appearance and fashionable attire, there was an almost feral quality to her, a quality that surged to the surface when she found herself frustrated or inconvenienced. And so, with one swift stride, Miss Chartier unleashed a vicious kick towards a particularly sensitive part of Wilde's anatomy, causing him to crumble to the floor gibbering in agony as the gun dropped from his nerveless fingers.

Picking the gun up, Miss Chartier pressed it against Wilde's temple. "Enough! If I hear one more cynical piece of wit, one more dry observation or droll comment, I swear to God I will kill you!"

Wilde was in no position to object or even speak, so Miss Chartier turned and addressed Van Gogh. "Vincent, gather your things. I must get out of this madhouse. We are going back to Arles so that you can paint for me day and night."

"Do you mean it, my love?"

"Of course, my sweet! With Paul gone, it will be just us two, and I shall put candles in your hat so you can paint your beautiful dreams beneath the starry sky."

"Ya, of course, my darling!"

Moving with more speed than I would have considered him capable of, Van Gogh disappeared back into my bedroom to get his valise. I rather liked the sound of Miss Chartier's last remark to Van Gogh, and so I brought out my notebook to write it down for future reference, only to have Miss Chartier pluck the notebook from my hand a moment later.

"No, no, no, Dr. Watson. If I might offer a bit of advice, do not imagine for one moment that you can write up this case for publication."

"What? I'll write whatever I please, thank you very much! This is England! And your nefarious scheme to exploit these poor artists needs to be exposed!"

"Ah, but exposure is a tricky thing, is it not? Should you feel compelled to tell your tale, then I feel certain that I would feel compelled to tell mine..."

"By all means! Publish and be damned!"

"...of a certain consulting detective who lives a life of drugs and debauchery with a known blackmailer by the name of Irene Adler. In other words, if you expose my scheme, I shall most assuredly expose yours."

At that, she handed me my notebook back, and I realised with a twinge of disappointment that she was right. This was not a case that could ever appear in the pages of "The Strand Magazine."

"She's good," remarked Miss Adler.

"Her father would be proud," agreed Holmes.

"*Merci beaucoup*," nodded Miss Chartier as Van Gogh emerged from my bedroom carrying his travelling case. A moment later he was wearing his hat and coat and clearly anxious to get back to Arles with Miss Chartier.

"I am ready, *ma chérie*. But..." Van Gogh scuttled closer to Miss Chartier and whispered urgently in her ear.

"But of course! Choose whichever you please, my darling."

Van Gogh quickly picked up one of the paintings. "I must have the Gauguin!"

"Hang on!" I objected. "Miss Adler purchased those! At least, I think she did..."

Turning to Miss Adler, she merely shrugged. "No matter. They were in the bargain bin."

"Then since I do not wish to clutter up your very charming rooms, I shall take the other two paintings as well." Miss Chartier directed Van Gogh with her hand. "Vincent, bring them along."

At that, I heard Wilde clearing his throat. "Actually, I wouldn't mind the Lautrec, if you don't mind. I'm rather fond of old Tripod."

Miss Chartier turned a calculating eye on Wilde. "And in exchange, you'll forgive my little knock on the head?"

"Done."

Wilde proceeded to pick up the painting by Lautrec as Van Gogh gathered up the Seurat. Seeing our last chance to hold Miss Chartier accountable for her actions, I mounted one final protest.

"Seriously? That was assault and battery, Wilde! You could press charges!"

"Oh no," Wilde waved my objections away with a languid gesture, "you should always forgive your enemies, Watson. Nothing annoys them more."

While I appreciated this final witty salvo from Wilde, he may as well have prodded at Miss Chartier with a sharp stick, as she turned and aimed her gun at him.

"Stop it!"

Perhaps realising that he would be helpless to prevent himself from uttering further witticisms if he stayed any longer, Wilde immediately made his way to the door, apologising the entire way, and then he was gone, his footsteps clattering down the stairs at speed.

Miss Chartier turned to Van Gogh, "Now let us take our leave."

Ushering Van Gogh before her, she waited until he was out the door and heading down the stairs, then turned back to us.

"I do not doubt that our paths will cross again, so this is not *adieu*, Mr. Holmes. Merely *au revoir*."

With that, she offered a very elegant curtsy, which Holmes returned with a bow. Miss Chartier and Miss Adler exchanged curt nods, and when Miss Chartier looked at me, I would swear that I saw a faint smile playing on her lips. It was almost as if she wanted to communicate something for my ears only, but then thinking better of it, she disappeared through the door, closing it behind her.

Miss Adler moved to the window and looked down at the street, no doubt seeing Van Gogh and Miss Chartier walking away together.

"He is in love with her. It's a shame she's the personification of evil."

Holmes was already leafing absentmindedly through a newspaper. "Well, you can't have everything in a relationship."

And it was only then, with all of our visitors departed and things seemingly getting back to normal, that I noticed it. Why I hadn't seen it before I couldn't tell you, because it had been right there in front of my eyes the whole time. Now it was as apparent to me as if a herd of elephants had appeared and were walking down the middle of Baker Street. My painting of legendary British hero General "Chinese" Gordon was missing!

I quickly ran my eyes around the room, thinking that perhaps it had been moved for some reason, but then I came back to the quite obvious empty space on our wall. It was gone. Immediately, my suspicions ran to Miss Adler, who had never approved of the portrait, claiming that Gordon was nothing more than a mentally ill mercenary, but then I reasoned that given the bizarre and hectic nature of our day, stealthily removing pictures from our walls was likely not a priority for her.

"Holmes! Miss Adler!" I announced. "There has been a crime here! We've been burgled!" As they both turned their attention to me, I pointed to the wall. "Look! Here on this wall! This is where I had my painting of General 'Chinese' Gordon!

It's gone! That's what all this was about! It was a plot to steal my painting! And right under our very noses!"

If I expected Holmes and Miss Adler to share my alarm and spring into action, I was sorely disappointed. Holmes merely shook his head slightly as he continued to scan articles in "The Times." "No, Watson. Calm yourself. There has been no theft."

"No theft? Then where's my painting?"

"I would draw your attention to the curious incident of the Post-Impressionist painter during the daytime."

"What on earth are you talking about?" I exclaimed.

"It was Mr. Van Gogh who removed the painting from the wall. You and Irene had just left, and I was looking for some tobacco, when Van Gogh emerged from your room singing some kind of Dutch folk song."

Miss Adler and I looked at one another.

"Yes!" I said. "We heard him too as we stood outside."

"Well, he simply came in here, glanced around the room, apparently liked the look of your General Gordon painting, removed it from the wall, and took it with him."

"Took it? Took it where?"

Holmes pointed to my bedroom and I ran towards it. Sure enough, partially obscured by my bed and leaning against the wall was what I can only call the remains of my painting. A cry of pure despair escaped me as I picked it up and rushed back to show Holmes and Miss Adler.

"Look what he's done!"

I held the painting up for their consideration. Any and all traces of "Chinese" Gordon were completely effaced. They had been painted over, and instead of Gordon's calm visage staring back at me there was only the image of Vincent Van Gogh. For some reason he had donned his hat and coat, with the white bandage covering his wound still clearly visible, and he had chosen to depict himself with a pipe sticking out of his mouth. It was, in short, as ridiculous as it was hideous, and while I felt for the poor man and all of his troubles, it was abundantly clear why he had yet to sell a single painting, because who in their right mind would want such an abomination in their home?

"This is...it's vandalism, that's what it is! Pure vandalism!" As Holmes gently prised the painting from my grasp, I desperately began thinking about what I could do. Perhaps with the paint still fresh it could be removed? Or maybe I needed to wait until it dried so that it could be carefully scraped off and the image of General Gordon could be recovered. I didn't have time for any more thoughts along those lines, because to my utter astonishment, Holmes had hung the painting back up in its original position.

"Holmes!" I cried. "You can't possibly be serious! You don't mean to keep that there do you?"

Holmes backed up a step or two and Miss Adler joined him. They wrapped their arms around each other's waists and regarded the painting as if it were a rosy-cheeked newborn.

"Just for a day or two," said Holmes. "Where's the harm, eh? Call it a little souvenir of the case..."

There was really nothing for it but a stiff drink, and so I made my way to the tantalus and poured myself a brandy. "Now what the bloody hell am I supposed to do with that?"

Miss Adler glanced at me over her shoulder. "I would suggest that you follow Miss Chartier's example. Keep it. Who knows, in a few years it might be worth a pound or two."

As much as I appreciated Miss Adler's attempt at humour, it would take more than one brandy for me to see anything amusing about the entire episode. Emptying my glass, I proceeded to refill it as Holmes mused, "It really is a damned shame that you can't put all this into one of your adventures."

With my blood warming, I retorted, "Who says I can't? This is the greatest Sherlock Holmes story ever! The world must know!"

"But Watson, need I point out the repercussions alluded to by Miss Chartier?"

"I didn't say the world needs to know at this very moment."

At that, both Holmes and Miss Adler looked towards me with quizzical expressions. Not wanting to spend the rest of the evening being interrogated by two of the finest minds in England, I came to a decision.

"Actually, there is something I have been meaning to tell you, and I hope that you won't disapprove or become cross with me. But the fact of the matter is, I've been keeping a secret from both you. Whenever we have a case whose details might be, shall we say, inappropriate for today's readers, I write it down and put it in a battered tin despatch box that I keep at Cox and Company in Charing Cross for safekeeping."

"Watson, you cunning old devil!" said Holmes.

"So, 'The Amateur Mendicant Society?'" asked Miss Adler.

"Yes."

"And 'Ricoletti of the Club Foot and His Abominable Wife?'" enquired Holmes.

"Obviously. Perhaps one day, those stories will be considered suitable for future generations, just like this one..."

"And what will this story be called?" continued Holmes. "You know what you should do if you can't think of a title? Talk to your friend Wilde. He seems like a clever fellow. In fact, maybe he could help you write it. Add a bit more, I don't know, cleverness and humour."

Perhaps considering the look in my eye, the second brandy in my hand, and a sturdy walking stick in the near vicinity, Miss Adler turned Holmes by the shoulder. "Speaking of Oscar Wilde, I have a Wildean riddle for you, dear."

"Do you?" Holmes was like an alert spaniel who has been shown a piece of bacon. "I love riddles!"

"I know. So, what is the only way to get rid of temptation, Mr. Holmes?"

Holmes pondered this for a moment, but only a moment. "Why, to yield to it, Miss Adler."

One meaningful glance from Miss Adler later, and she was leading Holmes to their bedroom. Still, Holmes couldn't resist a Parthian shot. "Watson, you're on your own. You can't expect us to solve the mystery and write the story for you as well."

"I couldn't agree more."

Miss Adler picked up Holmes' violin and bow and held them out. "Play for me, darling."

"Of course, my love."

And with that, they entered their bedroom, the door was firmly closed, and I was left to ponder what might be a suitable title for this case. Nothing immediately sprang to mind, but I had no intention of bring the topic up with Wilde, because no matter what sort of brilliant notion he might have, I knew I would never hear the end of it if I took his suggestion. In instances such as these, I find it helpful to go over my notes, and so I brought out my notebook to leaf through it for ideas.

Upon opening it, it wasn't a word or phrase that jumped out at me, it was quite literally Van Gogh's ear. It gave me something of a jolt to see it sitting there between the pages, scabbed and bloody, and I began to understand the reason behind Miss Chartier's small smile in my direction as she was leaving. Somehow, when she had snatched my notebook away to warn me against writing this story, she had used a bit of sleight of hand to slide Van Gogh's ear between the pages.

Still, as I sat there looking at it, I began to feel the stirrings of an idea—"The Adventure of...the Elusive Ear." Immediately, I liked the sound of it, and the more that I rolled it around in my head, the more I felt convinced that I had landed upon the perfect title. Yes, perhaps it had a touch of absurdity about it, because one doesn't normally consider ears to be all that elusive, but it seemed to fit the case beautifully. Besides, the great nonsense poet Edward Lear had passed away earlier in the year, and it would be my subtle homage to his whimsical and charming genius. From the bedroom, I could hear Holmes playing a passage from Jules Massenet's opera "Manon," and suitably inspired, began to pen the first draft of the tale you now have in your hands.

"It was in late December, 1888, and I had just awoken, quite refreshed after...a good night's sleep..."

The End.

Lightning Source UK Ltd.
Milton Keynes UK
UKHW020628010421
381362UK00007B/128